THE BRITTLENESS DEBT

Jacob E. Williams

ISBN: 979-8-9962187-1-4

Published by Stillwater Books

Optimization without redundancy is a loan from time.
Efficiency is a loan from time.
Every shaved margin, every removed buffer, every elegant dependency, all a loan from time.
And time always collects.

TABLE OF CONTENTS

PART I:
THE FRICTION OF CREEP

Chapter 1:
The Sensor Network

Systems Panoramic

The regional water table for Sub-District 4-A dropped three centimeters over twenty-four hours. On the state utility dashboard, the administrative status indicator for the Lorton pumping station remained solid green. The automated servers processed ninety-two thousand automated maintenance pings, filed them into local cache files, and cleared the log queues. The pressure drop was invisible on the public network.

Scene Core (Leo POV)

Leo adjusted the copper shielding around the main router housing with the edge of a flat screwdriver, pressing the mesh tight against the salvaged aluminum bracket until the metal stopped flexing under his thumb. It smelled of old solder, dust, and the faint resin sweetness that heated circuit boards gave off after running all day. On the desktop monitor, four columns of green text updated every three seconds, pulling live voltage data from the solar arrays on the garage roof and packet loss reports from the cul-de-sac mesh nodes.

Everything looked stable, which was exactly why Leo trusted the numbers more than the feeling in the room. The neighborhood mesh network was humming at ninety-eight percent efficiency, connecting twelve houses with encrypted low-power radio lines. Node latency remained under twelve milliseconds. Two driveway cameras were down, but both houses had reported that manually. The data was telling the truth, at least where it could still see.

The garage had become half workshop, half command post over the last year. A rack of salvaged routers sat on a pine shelf beside jars of stripped copper wire sorted by gauge. Two marine batteries rested in a spill tray under the bench with their charge controllers blinking in orderly sequence. On the pegboard above the monitor hung crimpers, hose clamps, a brass float valve Art had given Leo without explanation, and a laminated hand-drawn map of the cul-de-sac annotated with node locations and backup relay paths. Leo liked the map because it made the street feel legible.

Out in the street, ordinary life was still trying to impersonate itself. A lawn service truck downshifted somewhere beyond the ridge. A dog barked twice and was answered by another farther away. One of the older smart sprinklers on the next block hissed on for its timed cycle even though the grass beneath it had already gone half-brown. The neighborhood still sounded operational, which made failure harder to hear.

Elena walked into the garage, her boots clicking against the bare concrete. She dropped a heavy ring of keycards onto the workbench hard enough to make a spool of cat-five cable roll an inch.

"The hospital logistics grid is lagging by two hours," she said. She did not sit down. She stood over Leo's shoulder, still wearing her clinic badge and the look she got when things had started failing in ways administration would call temporary until they became fatal. "The pharmaceutical manifest from Richmond is stuck in queue. The state software won't let me release the local insulin reserves without the digital handshake from the central server."

Leo opened the county route monitor and checked the wider traffic map. The commercial backbone looked thin at the edge of the district, green nodes blinking farther apart than they had last week. "The main internet pipe is choking at the county line," Leo said. "The servers are dropping packets. It is an external routing failure."

Elena leaned closer to the monitor. The blue-white light cut the exhaustion under her eyes into harder lines. She had started doing that recently, reading screens the way Art read valves, as if enough attention might make a machine confess what it was hiding.

Leo pointed at a small secondary window in the lower corner of the display. It showed a line graph tracking the water pressure from the main coming off Silverbrook Road.

The curve had a slight downward slant, shallow enough to ignore if you wanted to keep believing in ordinary days.

"The automated municipal bot says the line is fine," Leo said. "It refreshed the status ten minutes ago."

"The city is losing staff, Leo. The bots just repeat the last valid telemetry they recorded before the personnel left." Elena touched the frame of the monitor with two fingers. "If that pressure curve drops below thirty pounds per square inch, the hospital booster pumps will cavity. They will pull vacuum and burn out their seals."

The word *cavity* made Leo think of empty volume forming inside a pipe where water ought to be, a clean invisible violence. They pulled up the neighborhood alert panel and set a new threshold. The command line accepted the change instantly. That felt reassuring in a way it should not have. "I am setting up a local alarm. If the pressure drops another point, the mesh network will page everyone on the cul-de-sac."

Outside, a passing truck hit a seam in the road and the window glass jittered in its frame. Then another sound rose through the floorboards of the garage, sharper and more regular, a rhythmic thumping that seemed to come from the house next door. It was not traffic. It was mechanical. Heavy. Wrong.

Leo looked up from the screen. The sound came again, a hydraulic piston struggling against air. "He's running his manual pump again."

Elena followed Leo's glance toward the side window. Through it, Art's basement well vent pipe was just visible against the brick wall, trembling slightly with each pulse. "He thinks he hears something in the pipes," she said. She picked up her keycards, her face tightening as she looked back toward the street. "Go see what he's measuring. I have to get back to the clinic before the automated security gates lock down for the evening shift."

Systems Panoramic

The local water line sustained a sudden pressure spike of twelve pounds per square inch as an air pocket moved through the secondary main. The digital telemetry node on the street valve remained static, transmitting a pre-recorded loop of standard operational data to the central county database. The database registered the event as normal.

Chapter 2:
Air in the Lines

Systems Panoramic

The velocity of fluid through the secondary six-inch cast-iron main on Silverbrook Road decreased to zero point four meters per second. This reduction allowed suspended iron oxide particles to settle into the bottom invert of the pipe, forming a heavy, abrasive slurry. At the treatment plant three miles upstream, automated chemical feed pumps continued to inject sodium hypochlorite at maximum capacity, compensating for a telemetry error in the primary flow meter.

Scene Core (Art POV)

Art kept his right hand flat against the copper intake pipe rising from the basement concrete. The metal vibrated with a frantic, uneven chatter that told him exactly how much air was trapped in the municipal line. He counted the seconds between the thumps without looking at a clock. The intervals were shrinking. That meant the pressure collapse was moving closer, not away.

The basement was close and damp, built for storage rather than comfort. One pull-chain bulb threw a yellow cone of light over the workbench and left the back corners in shadow. Along the far wall sat old treatment manuals, coffee cans of brass fittings, a hand auger, and three milk crates full of obsolete meter housings he had never found it in himself to throw away. The room smelled of wet concrete, cold iron, pipe dope, and the hard chemical sting rising from the vented water line.

He picked up a heavy adjustable wrench from the canvas roll on his stool and loosened the packing nut on the primary isolation valve by a quarter turn. A pale jet of high-pressure water hissed through the threads, spraying his knuckles and instantly filling the room with the sharp chlorinated stench of swimming pool bleach. The water ran cold into his sleeve.

"They're drowning it," Art muttered.

He tightened the nut until the flow dropped to a controlled drip into a glass beaker. Then he reached for a cardboard box of digital test strips salvaged from the filtration facility two years ago. The box was soft at the corners from age and cellar damp. He dipped one strip into the sample and held it under the bulb. The paper turned a deep, bruised purple within two seconds. Free chlorine above eight parts per million. Twice the legal limit. High enough to chew through membranes, seals, and anything fragile the system pretended would last forever.

The basement stairs creaked. Leo stood on the bottom step, holding a handheld tablet inside a thick rubber frame. The screen cast a weak green wash across their jaw and knuckles.

"The mesh network flagged your pump activity, Art," Leo said. "The dashboard shows a minor pressure fluctuation on our side of the street."

"Your dashboard is watching a phantom," Art said. He did not look up from the beaker. "Smell that? That is municipal panic. The treatment operators have walked out, and the system is running on a dead-man's loop. The automated pumps are dumping raw chemical to kill whatever is growing in the dead ends."

Leo came off the step and walked to the bench, tapping the screen. "The county status node still shows the treatment plant is operational. The green indicator is live."

Art twisted the wrench until the hiss dropped to a steady rhythmic drip. "The indicator is live because the server hasn't crashed yet. The water inside the pipe doesn't care about the server. The water is telling you the intake line is cavitating. The city pool is empty, Leo. The mains are sucking air from the high points on the ridge."

He set the wrench down, wiped his wet fingers on his canvas trousers, and pulled a small leather-bound notebook from his pocket. The pages were yellowed at the edges, filled with hand-drawn schematics of the Lorton water grid from 1998, cross-referenced with valve locations that had never been integrated into the county's digital map. With a blunt pencil he recorded the chlorine level, the pulse interval, and the time in one line of cramped capitals: *16:12. 8.2 PPM. PRESSURE FLUCTUATING.*

Leo looked at the purple strip on the bench, then back at the tablet, as if the numbers on one ought to have apologized to the other. "If the chlorine is that high, the automated reverse-osmosis units in the neighborhood will foul. The membranes will degrade within forty-eight hours."

"Then tell your neighbors to isolate their smart-tanks manually," Art said, closing the notebook with a sharp snap. "Put it on your mesh network. Tell them to use their hands and turn the brass valves clockwise until they bottom out. If they wait for an app to update the status, they'll be drinking bleach by morning."

Leo hesitated, still looking between the strip and the screen. Art could almost hear the boy sorting reality by which source looked cleaner. The pipe thumped again under Art's palm. The answer was in the wall, not the dashboard.

Systems Panoramic

The residual chlorine gas in the dead-end lines began to corrode the synthetic rubber gaskets inside forty-two residential water meters along the cul-de-sac. The micro-rotors inside the meters, designed to transmit usage data via low-frequency radio, stalled as the polymer expanded. On the central utility network, the affected houses quietly dropped from the active monitoring database, registered by the server as vacant properties.

Chapter 3:
The Broken Manifest

Systems Panoramic

The central procurement server in Richmond initiated an automated database sweep of regional medical repositories. Finding seventy-two unresolved transport manifests from the past forty-eight hours, the system re-allocated three hundred tactical supply shipments to Tier-1 federal consolidation nodes. The algorithm categorized Sub-District 4-A as a low-density buffer zone. The change in status automatically generated a public safety alert across all municipal screens.

Scene Core (Elena POV)

Elena kept her eyes on the digital inventory ledger. The screen threw a cold blue light across her desk, highlighting the row of empty plastic storage bins stacked against the clinic wall and the water rings drying beneath them like pale target marks. She clicked the refresh button. The loading spinner rotated six times, froze, and then displayed the same error message: *Manifest 904-B: Pending Institutional Verification.*

The clinic felt wrong in the way a body feels wrong before it is sick enough to collapse. The overhead fluorescents still worked, but one tube above the medicine counter was beginning to strobe at the edges. The manual sink in the corner dripped into a steel basin because the pressure regulator no longer held steady. On the far wall, laminated infection-control posters curled away from the cinderblock where the adhesive had dried out years ago. The room was clean by ordinary standards. By Elena's standards, it already looked abandoned.

"The Richmond distribution dock isn't answering the phone," Sarah said. She was leaning against the doorframe, her nurse's scrubs stained with water marks from the manual clinic sink. A clipboard was tucked against her hip, and the top page was warped from repeated handling. "The dialysis unit on the third floor has enough concentrate for tomorrow morning. That is our absolute ceiling."

Elena clicked the manifest again and opened the freight routing pane. Three trucks were visible on the map as stationary green squares, idling in a holding yard outside Richmond. The line was open. The inventory existed. The problem was not matter. The problem was permission.

"They cleared the freight line an hour ago," Elena said. She did not look up from the display. "The trucks are sitting at the distribution yard. The system simply won't release the gate locks because the regional compliance officer didn't log in to sign the digital transfer vouchers."

Sarah pushed off the doorframe and stepped into the room. "Can we send a vehicle down there with a paper order? A stamped one? Anything they can physically hand to a guard?"

"The yard is automated, Sarah. The perimeter fences are hooked into the state grid. If you don't have a valid QR authorization code on your phone, the gate sensors flag the truck as a security threat. The logistics system is completely blind to our physical inventory."

She said it flatly, but the sentence carried twenty years of fatigue. She had spent her career standing in exactly that seam between need and procedure, translating shortages into tolerable language for people who wanted a clean dashboard more than a functioning floor.

A dialysis alarm sounded faintly somewhere down the hall, then cut off. A cart wheel squeaked over cracked tile. Someone in the waiting room coughed into a paper towel with the long, hollow force of dehydration. Elena did not move from the desk. She opened the backup inventory tab and checked insulin reserves, saline bags, antibiotic counts, and the dwindling boxes of water purification tablets she had been quietly holding back from central reporting for weeks.

The columns looked stable until you noticed the dates. That was how these systems failed now. They simply stopped replenishing.

A loud chime sounded from the tablet on Elena's desk. The screen flickered, overriding the inventory ledger with a stark gray graphic displaying the state seal.

The text was written in the flat, bureaucratic style of a permanent administrative directive:

REGIONAL PUBLIC SAFETY NOTICE: SUB-DISTRICT 4-A

Effective immediately, municipal utility maintenance and emergency medical response infrastructure within this sector will be consolidated into the Potomac Regional Security Camp (PRSC), located forty-two miles north. Citizens remaining in outlying districts are advised to register all personal medical, caloric, and energy assets via the state portal. Failure to register within seventy-two hours will result in the suspension of all baseline electronic ration allocations.

Elena sat back in her chair. The plastic creaked under her weight. For one second she let the language settle exactly as written, because she had spent enough years inside institutional retreat to know the vocabulary of abandonment when it arrived in official fonts.

"They are pulling the line back," Sarah whispered, her face pale in the blue light of the monitor. "They want us to pack up the clinic and move the patients into the barracks."

"The camp doesn't have sixty dialysis chairs, Sarah. It has a tent grid and a central distribution kitchen," Elena said. Her fingers tightened around her keycard lanyard until the plastic edge bit into her palm. "They aren't expanding services. They are shrinking the perimeter so they only have to maintain one set of transformers and one water treatment line."

Sarah stared at the notice. "What about the insulin? What about the unit upstairs? What about people who can't survive transport?"

Elena did not answer right away. She was already reading the directive the way a hostile administrator would read it, looking for the hidden mechanism. Register all assets. Suspend baseline electronic ration allocations. Centralized security. It was not an evacuation notice. It was a requisition framework with softer verbs.

Her phone buzzed in her pocket. It was a text message from Leo via the neighborhood mesh network, bypassing the failing commercial towers: *Art was right about the mains. The smart-tanks are fouling. The pressure at the cul-de-sac valve just dropped to eighteen PSI.*

Elena looked from the state alert on her tablet to the empty supply bins on the floor, then to the backup insulin cooler humming under the desk. The administrative structure she had spent twenty years navigating was retreating from the landscape, leaving behind a digital command to comply and a set of forms designed to locate whatever useful goods remained.

She reached over the desk, opened the clinic server settings, and pulled up the external sync permissions. A list of authorized state endpoints appeared in green. She shut them down one by one.

"We aren't filling out the registration portal," Elena said, her voice dropping to a flat, decisive tone. "If we log our inventory into their database, the system will automatically flag our insulin and water storage for requisition to the central camp. Shut down the external sync on the clinic server. We run local records from now on."

Systems Panoramic

The municipal cellular tower on Silverbrook Road adjusted its directional antenna array to prioritize the government transport corridor two miles east. Residential bandwidth inside the cul-de-sac dropped by eighty-five percent. The local mesh nodes detected the loss and rerouted internal traffic through the low-frequency radio bridges built in Leo's garage.

Chapter 4:
The Seasonal Freeze

Systems Panoramic

The thermal load on Sub-District 4-A's primary electrical substation exceeded mechanical safety parameters at eleven point four degrees Fahrenheit. The automated circuit breakers tripped three times, attempting to isolate a cascading ground fault along the buried lines on Silverbrook Road. On the fourth attempt, the sulfur hexafluoride gas switches failed to extinguish the arc. The copper busbars melted within four seconds, terminating electrical service to seven hundred residential lots.

Scene Core (Leo POV)

Leo watched the battery indicators on the dashboard die one by one. The smart-home wall units in the garage clicked, their internal relays dropping open as the utility grid fell to zero volts. For three minutes the backup lithium bank held the system load. The display dimmed, brightened once, then went gray.

The silence in the garage was absolute, broken only by the dry hiss of sleet hitting the metal roof and the soft settling ticks of hardware cooling faster than it was designed to cool. Leo could hear their own breathing now, thin in the cold. The smart thermostat display on the wall blinked once and died with the rest of the system.

They picked up a headlamp from the charging cradle. Dead. The smart charger had failed to complete its cycle before the outage. Leo found a mechanical hand-cranked flashlight in a drawer under a box of old signal wire, wound the plastic lever thirty times until the gears bit, and stepped out into the dark.

The cul-de-sac was unrecognizable under four inches of frozen crust. The streetlamps were black stalks against the gray sky. Sleet clicked against the hood of a parked sedan already frosting over at the windshield seams. A child's bicycle lay on its side at the edge of a drift, half-buried. Across the street, the front door to Art's house stood open, a faint amber glow flickering against the snow in the hallway.

By the time Leo crossed the street, their jeans were wet to the shin. The cold had a way of climbing. It moved through the boots, into the socks, into the bones above the ankle. They went down through the cellar door into the basement heat and the smell of wood smoke so fast it almost felt like falling.

Twelve neighbors were crowded into the small workshop, sitting on overturned plastic crates and toolboxes. The center of the room was dominated by Art's old cast-iron wood stove, its flue pipe glowing a dull red where it met the masonry chimney. Wet gloves steamed on the workbench. Meltwater collected beneath boots in black half-moons on the concrete. The air smelled of wood ash, wet wool, kerosene, and the sour edge of fear. Someone had set two infants together in a laundry basket lined with towels near the warm side of the room.

A neighbor named Miller held up a blank smartphone screen as if it had personally failed him. "The digital notice just popped up before the tower died," he said. "It said the evacuation buses are stopping at the high school. If we don't clear out by midnight, they're cutting the electronic food tokens."

"The high school is unheated, Miller," Elena said. She was standing by the woodbox, her winter coat zipped to her chin, one hand braced on the wall as if she had been moving all evening without stopping. "They don't have blankets for three hundred people, and they don't have water. The county turned off the treatment plant pumps four hours ago."

"We can't stay here in the dark," Miller said, his voice rising until two children by the stairs went still. "The indoor plumbing is going to freeze by morning. My smart thermostat said the house temperature was already down to forty-five."

Art picked up an iron poker and raked the coals inside the stove. A shower of sparks rose against the firebrick. He did not turn around when he answered.

"Your thermostat is a brick now, Miller. Your plumbing will freeze if you leave the water sitting in the lines. Go home, close your main internal valve in the crawlspace, and open every faucet in the house. Drain the pipes into buckets. If the water freezes inside the copper, the tubes will split like sausages."

He pointed with the poker toward the stairwell without looking up. "Pull the trap under every sink if you know how. If you don't know how, leave it and come back here before the pipes burst. Don't guess at plumbing in the dark."

"And then what?" Miller asked. "What do we drink on Tuesday?"

Art pointed a blunt finger toward the corner of the basement, where three fifty-gallon blue polymer drums sat linked by galvanized pipe. A manual brass pitcher pump was bolted to the top of the first barrel. The setup looked primitive beside the dead tablets and dark phones in people's hands, which was exactly why it still mattered.

"That is ninety-five percent pure well water," Art said. "It doesn't use a grid, and it doesn't use a server. It uses a leather gasket and human arms. If you want a gallon, you come down here and you crank the handle until your bucket is full."

Leo looked at the small tablet in their hands, still running on its emergency battery. The local mesh nodes were still pinging one another, their green status lights forming a tiny isolated island of data on the map, completely detached from the dead regional infrastructure beyond the ridge. The little cluster looked less like control than like a heartbeat too small for the body it belonged to.

"The mesh is still up," Leo said to the room. "I can link the battery sensors from the garage to Art's well pump. We can track how much water we use and budget it across the twelve houses."

Heads turned toward the tablet. Not because anyone fully trusted it anymore, Leo realized, but because people still wanted something measurable to hold onto while everything else went dark.

Before Elena spoke, the room showed its fracture openly. Mrs. Albright had already bundled two blankets around her grandchildren and was whispering that the buses at least had roofs. Miller kept asking whether anyone had seen county headlights on the ridge road, as if repetition might turn rumor into transport. A boy near the stove began to cry because his mother had told him to keep his shoes on in case they had to run. In the corner, one man quietly folded a road map along the old commuter route north and slid it into his coat pocket before Art could see. The room was not waiting for leadership. It was beginning to shear into private exits.

Elena looked at Leo, then at the neighbors packed around the stove, then at the barrels in the corner and the wood stacked shoulder high by the stair wall. She was counting more than gallons. She was counting how long fear could be organized before it turned into flight.

"We stay," Elena said. Her voice was not loud, but the room quieted around it. "We don't register for the camp, and we don't board the buses. We have the well, we have the wood, and we have the ledger. We build our own line here."

Systems Panoramic

The central administrative server in Richmond recorded a total communication timeout for Sub-District 4-A at twenty-three point fifteen hours. The system automatically flagged the entire postal code as an unpopulated zone, shifting its resource allocation algorithms to focus exclusively on the managed perimeter of the Potomac Regional Security Camp. The residential sector was cleared from the active maintenance queue.

PART II: THE LOGISTICS OF HOPE

Chapter 5:
Breaking the Asphalt

Systems Panoramic

The ground temperature in Sub-District 4-A stabilized at fifty-four degrees Fahrenheit. Without municipal street sweepers or chemical weed control, the seeds of common dandelion, chicory, and wild mustard germinated within the microscopic fissures of the suburban roadway. The expansion of the root structures exerted an upward pressure of ninety pounds per square inch against the aggregate base course, widening the cracks by three millimeters over twenty days.

Scene Core (Elena POV)

Elena wiped the sweat from her eyes with the back of a mud-caked canvas glove. The spring sun was thin, but the physical labor of the pry-bar had turned her thermal shirt into a damp weight against her shoulders. Fine gray dust clung to the hair at her temples and settled into the crease of her elbows each time she bent.

The cul-de-sac no longer looked like a street. It looked like a quarry cut into a neighborhood. Chunks of asphalt lay stacked in black, jagged piles along the curb. A wheelbarrow with one bent handle sat half-filled with broken aggregate. Someone had stretched mason's twine between two rebar stakes to keep the first planting row straight, though the line already sagged in the heat.

Two feet away, Miller swung a twelve-pound sledgehammer down onto the asphalt with both hands. The tool hit the blacktop with a dull, bone-jarring thud, chipping away a piece of stone aggregate the size of a fist. The impact vibrated through the soles of Elena's boots. He drew the hammer back again more slowly this time, his breath snagging in his throat before the next swing.

On the far side of the circle, Sarah and two teenagers were on their knees pulling root mat from the first exposed strip of soil and shaking pale worms out of it into a bucket. Leo was at the garage threshold with a tablet and a paper clipboard both tucked under one arm, trying to keep the labor roster dry from a burst hose someone had rigged to rinse the dust off salvageable loam. Every task on the street now had to be done twice, once by hand and once by count.

"We need to clear another twelve linear feet before sundown," Elena said, her voice dry from the dust. "The potato sets need to go in while the soil is still damp from the rain."

"The base stone under this layer is like concrete," Miller panted, leaning his forehead against the hickory handle of the hammer. His palms were blistered through his work gloves, the raw pink skin showing where the fabric had worn thin. "My hands are locking up, Elena. We've been at this since six."

Elena planted the point of her six-foot steel bar into a fresh fracture line and rocked it until she felt the tip bite. "We need sixty pounds of caloric yield per household to hit the minimum baseline Leo calculated." She leaned her entire weight backward, using a chunk of broken concrete as a fulcrum. The bar flexed. The asphalt groaned, lifted two inches, and then snapped with a hard crack like a pistol shot. A sheet of blacktop peeled up, exposing pale, compacted fill beneath it.

The shock ran through her shoulders and down into her wrists. For a second the old hospital part of her tried to rise above the scene and turn the street into a staffing problem. But the road answered only to leverage, fatigue, and the angle of steel.

Across the cleared patch of gray earth, Art sat on an upturned five-gallon bucket. He was using an old iron file to sharpen the edge of a square-point shovel. He did not offer to lift a bar, but his eyes never left the excavation line.

"You're digging too deep on the north side, Elena," Art said, the file scraping rhythmically against the steel blade. *Scritch. Scritch.* "The road crew used a heavy limestone fill under that section to level the slope back in ninety-five. If you mix that rock into the topsoil, your potatoes will scab.

Keep your trench four inches closer to the curb where the sandy loam is clean."

Elena straightened her back, hearing her spine click. Sweat had run down under the waistband of her work pants and dried there as grit. "We are short on labor, Art. If you took a turn with the pick, we could keep the trench straight."

Art laid the shovel across his knees. "My back won't handle the swing, Elena. And a broken old man is just another mouth that needs extra medicine you don't have. I am saving you the calories of digging out dead stone."

She wanted to answer him, but another hammer blow landed to her left and the street shuddered again. The whole operation had acquired a rhythm over the last week: strike, pry, lift, shovel, sort, drag, stack. A subdivision teaching itself how to behave like a work crew. Some people had the stamina for it. Some only had fear. Most had both.

A sharp, metallic clatter echoed from the edge of the cul-de-sac.

The sound was wrong enough that Elena knew, before she turned, it was not just dropped steel.

A neighbor named Tommy had been using a heavy iron wedge to split the larger chunks of roadbed. The wedge had slipped under the hammer stroke. Tommy was on his knees now, clutching his left shin, his face turning a gray, greasy color under his sunburn. The hammer had gone rolling into the gutter, leaving a crescent track in the dust.

Elena dropped her pry-bar and ran across the broken asphalt. Loose fragments shifted under her boots. Somebody shouted Tommy's name. Somebody else shouted for water, uselessly, as if this were heatstroke and not blunt force and open bone.

The edge of the twelve-pound sledge had glanced off the steel wedge and struck Tommy's lower leg. Through the torn denim of his jeans, the white edge of the tibia was visible, protruding through a jagged three-inch tear in the skin. Blood was beginning to well up, thick and dark, pooling in the dust of the road base and turning it instantly to paste.

"Don't move, Tommy," Elena said, her operational training flattening her voice into a calm instrument. "Sarah. Trauma bag from the porch. Now. Miller, get back and give me light."

She knelt in the dirt, ignoring the sharp stones cutting into her knees through the canvas. Heat was coming off the roadbed. She pulled a pair of trauma shears from her belt and slit the denim up to the thigh. The bone fracture was complete. The muscle tissue around it had already started to swell. Small black grains of road grit were embedded in the wet red surface like filings pressed into grease.

Tommy made a small, breathless sound when she exposed the wound, not quite a scream, more the noise a man made when the body understood something the mind had not caught up to yet.

"Is it... is it bad?" Tommy whispered, his eyes rolling back toward his skull.

Sarah dropped to one knee beside her with the trauma bag. Elena tore it open, took a sterile abdominal pad, and pressed it firmly against the wound to check the bleeding. "It is a clean break, but the skin is open," she said. "We have twenty-one doses of broad-spectrum cephalexin left in the clinic safe. This wound has road dirt in the marrow. We will have to use five of those doses just to prevent osteomyelitis."

She said the number out loud because the street had to hear it. Nothing cost only pain anymore. Everything also cost inventory.

She looked up at the circle of neighbors gathering around the pool of blood. Miller was shaking, his hands still twitching from the vibration of the hammer. Sarah had gone pale under the dust on her cheeks. Leo stood at the back, holding the electronic tablet, the screen displaying a pristine green spreadsheet titled *Agricultural Caloric Projections.*

The spreadsheet had no cell for a compound fracture. It had no column for bone infection or the permanent loss of a functioning adult worker during planting week. The model remained clean while the real world on the pavement grew bloody, heavy, and expensive.

"Get the stretcher from the garage," Elena told Miller. Her voice left no room for hesitation. "We are moving him to my living room. Boil two gallons of well water and strip the clean sheets off the line. I need a splint board, towels, and somebody to clear my dining table now."

Systems Panoramic

The automated medical logistics server in Richmond processed a routine security update, renewing its encryption protocols for thirty-two district hospitals. Finding no operational data transmission or administrative activity logs from the Lorton clinic node for ninety consecutive days, the system permanently archived the clinic's digital identification key, categorizing the physical facility as an abandoned asset.

Chapter 6:
The Small Temptation

Systems Panoramic

The total caloric reserve of the twelve households on the cul-de-sac decreased to three hundred and forty-two thousand kilocalories. This inventory represented forty-one days of baseline survival rations if distributed equally among the thirty-four remaining individuals. The loss of Tommy from the labor pool reduced the community's daily physical work capacity by eight point three percent, increasing the projected time required to complete the agricultural beds by four days.

Scene Core (Leo POV)

Leo sat at the workbench, tapping the screen with a stylus made from a plastic pen casing. The garage smelled of woodsmoke from the neighbor's chimney and the bitter, sharp scent of vinegar Elena was using to sterilize the sheets in Tommy's room next door. The vinegar kept cutting through everything else, through solder dust, damp concrete, and the faint sweet rot of potato peels left too long in a compost pail by the side door.

On the monitor, a new module of Leo's script was compiling. Lines of Python code scrolled down the screen in a rapid sequence of green text, then resolved into a cleaner interface than the one Leo had been using for garden tallies. Three panes sat side by side: household census, labor log, and caloric reserve. Beneath them, a fourth pane waited for output. The layout had the sterile neatness of a clinic form, and Leo liked that. It looked like something that could hold when people did not.

On the bench beside the keyboard lay the hand-written records Leo had fed into the script over the last two nights: names, ages, task hours, carried weight, injury restrictions, medication needs, and daily bucket counts from the well. A fine black line of graphite dust marked the heel of Leo's palm from moving between paper and machine. The data had come from bodies, arguments, and porch counts. On the screen, it no longer argued.

Since Tommy's fracture, the street had developed a new caution that the script did not know how to count. Hammer blows now came farther apart. People lifted broken asphalt as if the road itself might answer back. At dawn, Leo had watched Miller pause before handing a pry-bar to his eldest boy, testing the steel in his palm first as though weight had become a medical question. Even the labor logs reflected it indirectly, more incomplete shifts, more modified assignments, more minutes lost to standing still and looking at tools before using them.

"It is ready," Leo said as Elena walked into the garage. Her eyes were bloodshot, and her collar was damp with well water. One sleeve of her thermal shirt had been rolled to the elbow and forgotten there, exposing a forearm crosshatched with shallow scratches from hauling roadbed and splints.

"Tommy's fever is down to a hundred and one," Elena said, leaning against the edge of the tool chest. She looked at the display, and Leo saw the exact moment her shoulders dropped half an inch. "But Miller is refusing to work the afternoon shift. He says his back is thrown out from the sledgehammer, and the Davis family is complaining that the Miller house got three more potatoes than they did in the Thursday distribution."

As if to underline her point, voices drifted in through the open side window from the lane outside. Somebody was arguing about seed trays. Somebody else was counting jars. The whole neighborhood had begun to sound like books that would not reconcile.

"They got three more because the old tracking method was arbitrary," Leo said, clicking the mouse to initialize the new interface. The screen redrew in clean blocks. "The script solves the human friction. It is a linear optimization model."

Leo reached out and tapped the side of a salvaged plastic casing zip-tied to the garage door frame. Inside, a seven-inch liquid-crystal display from an old supermarket check-out terminal flickered with a dull green phosphor glare. Leo had wired the unit directly to an old Android phone running a terminal emulator, its camera lens aligned with a slot cut into the plywood casing at the gatepost. The script had already started taking shape in hardware.

"I finished mounting the scanner interface at the perimeter entrance this morning," Leo explained, scrolling through the device logs. "Household 3 and Household 11 already used their barcodes to clear their entry tokens for the tillage shift. The mechanical deadbolt on the gate clicks open for exactly forty-five seconds when a valid ID token is presented under the lens."

Elena stepped closer, her gaze tracking the rows of text on the master monitor. "And if the token is invalid?"

"The screen prints a red restriction code and the latch stays dead," Leo said, pointing to a terminal line marked *Log: Entry Denied - Node 14 (Davis).* "The neighbors aren't coming to your porch to beg for extra minutes anymore. They stand at the terminal, present the laminate card to the lens, and the machine tells them whether they've earned the clearance. It takes the negotiation out of the dirt."

"Show me the distribution queue for the rest of the street."

Leo pulled up the neighborhood panoramic array. The screen populated with twelve horizontal bars, each representing a house on the cul-de-sac.

"House 5 and House 9 are balancing their water draw down to the ounce," Leo said, tracing the data blocks with the stylus. "But look at the aggregate curve. The five households on the south side are running an average daily deficit of six percent because they are hauling graywater manually in five-gallon oil tubs instead of using the gravity-fed line. The model tracks that latency. It automatically throttles their morning flour weights to offset the energy deficit."

Elena stepped closer, her gaze tracking the columns. "Explain the logic."

Leo rotated the monitor slightly so she could see better. The casing gave off a faint static pop where one corner had been taped after the freeze. "I coded three specific input parameters," Leo said, pointing the stylus at the screen. "Caloric inventory, physical contribution hours, and biological dependency factors, like age, illness, and injury status. The script takes the raw data and outputs a daily distribution schedule. It removes the human element entirely."

Leo opened the labor pane. Rows of names appeared with shaded cells marking completed shifts, missed assignments, and modified duties. Tommy's row was grayed out with a medical restriction flag. Miller's row showed an incomplete afternoon labor block. The Davis family's row showed extra seed-sorting time and water-hauling work that had not been fully credited under Elena's paper method.

"Because Miller didn't complete his three-hour asphalt clearing slot yesterday," Leo said, tapping the highlighted line, "the script adjusted his family's allocation for this morning by four hundred calories. It reallocated those calories to the Davis house because they completed an extra hour of seed sorting and a second bucket rotation from the well."

Elena frowned. "Miller has three children, Leo. If you drop their baseline, they will notice it by noon."

"The children are protected by the dependency coefficient," Leo said. Leo opened a second sub-menu to show the ratio bands. "The reduction only hits Miller's adult portion. The model calculates the exact physiological cost of the work done and returns the exact fuel required to sustain it. If someone doesn't work, they don't burn the calories, so the reserve isn't wasted on them. It is perfectly efficient."

Elena said nothing for a moment. Leo watched her eyes move from the formula bands to the output pane, where the revised ration weights had already populated in smooth decimal values. Outside, the argument in the lane had shifted houses. A screen door struck shut. Then another. Then silence.

"Run yesterday's full census through it," Elena said.

Leo loaded the neighborhood file. The processor icon spun, then the lower pane filled with a distribution table: households, morning weights, evening supplements, labor call times, and protected medical exceptions. A second graph projected reserve stability through the next six weeks if compliance held above eighty-seven percent. The line was narrow, clean, and upward enough to feel like mercy.

Elena leaned one hand on the bench. Leo could see the exhaustion in the tendon standing out at her wrist. She had spent months absorbing every complaint personally, every ounce of grain becoming a face, every missed shift becoming a moral referendum on her porch. On the monitor, none of it looked personal anymore. It looked solvable.

"It takes the blame off our hands," Elena whispered.

Leo felt a small, private surge of relief at the words. "It doesn't care who anyone likes," Leo said. "The script doesn't care who is friends with whom. It only looks at total loop stability."

The cellar door clicked open. Art stood in the entryway, holding an empty five-gallon bucket by the steel handle. He looked first at the glowing display, then at Elena's face, and then at the neat ration table on the screen. Mud had dried in ridges along the sole of one boot. He had come in from the well, from a system that still had to be felt with the hands.

"You're letting the machine write the grocery list, I see," Art said, his voice flat.

"It isn't a grocery list, Art," Leo said, turning in the chair. "It is an objective resource tracker. It balances what we have against what we do. It ensures we don't run out of food before the potato harvest."

Art walked over to the workbench, his boots leaving dry crusts of dirt on the floor. He set the bucket down without taking his eyes off the monitor. The metal ring hit the concrete with a hard hollow note.

"The model doesn't know that Miller's youngest child has been sneaking half her breakfast to the dog because she's scared the animal is going to starve," Art said. "It doesn't know that Miller spent two hours last night sitting with Tommy so Elena could sleep. Where do those hours go on your screen, Leo?"

"The model can only calculate quantifiable data, Art," Leo said, their voice tightening despite the effort to keep it even. "If we manage this by emotion, we will run out of grain by mid-summer. The code is protecting us from ourselves."

For a moment no one moved. Then a fresh burst of argument rose outside, sharper now, and somebody knocked on the side door but did not enter. Elena looked toward the sound, then back at the monitor. The choice was already making itself attractive.

Elena took the stylus from Leo's hand and tapped the confirmation box on the screen. The printer on the shelf, wired into Leo's battery bank, began to click, spitting out a narrow strip of paper containing the morning's work assignments and exact ration weights. Each weight was rounded to the tenth. Each name sat on its own line. The machine made the list sound official simply by finishing it.

"Print the list, Leo," Elena said. Her voice had steadied. "We will hand it out at the gate during the eight o'clock census. If anyone has a complaint, tell them the allocation is determined by the community baseline script."

At eight o'clock the line formed by the southern gate in a silence that felt more bureaucratic than communal. Leo stood beside the printer tray with a stack of narrow paper slips warming their palm. Elena called each household by number, but after the first two distributions people stopped looking at her and began looking directly at the decimals. Miller read his slip once, then a second time, his mouth tightening not at Elena but at the tenth-place reduction beside his adult portion. Mrs. Albright asked whether the model had counted her husband's swollen hands as a medical variance or a labor deficit, and when Elena started to answer, Leo heard Henderson say from the back of the line, "If the script set it, arguing won't add an ounce." Household 3 left with a slightly heavier flour weight and the kind of relief that made them avoid House 7's eyes. By the fourth slip, the choreography had changed. The neighbors were no longer receiving food from Elena. They were receiving output from the machine, and carrying the paper away as if that alone had made it binding.

Systems Panoramic

The local mesh network transmitted forty-two data packets to the electronic locks on the communal food storage bay, updating the access permissions based on Leo's optimization script. The mechanical pins inside the secondary locks clicked into place, restricting entry to designated fulfillment hours. The lockwork functioned with absolute technical precision, independent of the growing silence in the houses across the pavement.

Chapter 7:
The Well and the Drift

Systems Panoramic

The subterranean static water level within the lower Potomac aquifer shifted to eighty-four feet below the ground surface line. The water column contained four hundred and twelve milligrams per liter of suspended silt particles, along with trace concentrations of iron bacteria. At the surface, a low-voltage solar pump drew twelve liters per minute through an old steel casing, moving the liquid into a two-tiered settlement system.

Scene Core (Art POV)

Art hung a zinc-plated plumb bob into the dark opening of the old well shaft. He let the braided nylon line slip through his calloused fingers until the brass weight hit the water surface with a faint metallic *clink*. The sound came up the casing half a beat late, smaller than it should have been. He pinched the wet line against his thumbnail, hauled it back into the noon light, and checked the markings darkened into the cord with India ink twenty years earlier.

"Eighty-four feet," Art said. He wiped the string with a piece of waste rag and glanced at the settlement tanks sweating in the heat beyond the wellhead. "The drawdown is accelerating. We're pulling two inches an hour out of the reserve pool because the garden beds are sucking the tanks dry faster than the aquifer wants to recover."

The well yard behind the houses had once been decorative, little more than scrub grass and a capped municipal relic half-hidden under volunteer sumac. Now it had become the mechanical heart of the cul-de-sac. Two plastic settlement tanks stood on cinderblock risers linked by hose and threaded steel fittings. A low-voltage solar pump clicked on and off beneath a plywood rain shield. The ground around the casing was already churned to a gray paste by boots, wheelbarrows, and spilled slurry.

Leo was kneeling in the mud beside the wellhead, wiring a plastic digital turbidity sensor into a splice box on the intake line. The little optical eye sat clean and bright inside its molded housing, far too delicate for the kind of water moving below it. A coil of stripped copper wire lay on a feed sack by Leo's knee. Their fingers were quick and precise, clean except for the gray smear of electrical tape adhesive and the mud creeping slowly into the seams of their sneakers.

"The system is matching the predictive evaporation index," Leo said without looking up. They twisted the signal wires together, checked the polarity against a hand-drawn diagram, then tightened the terminal screws with a stubby insulated driver. "The sensor will track the clarity of the water in real time. If the silt level rises above twenty nephelometric units, the automated solenoid valve closes and protects the domestic filters before the tanks foul."

Art crouched at the casing and looked down into the shadowed shaft. The smell rising from it was cold stone, wet iron, and the faint organic rot that lived in old groundwater. He could hear the pump impellers singing too high under load. "The sensor will get blind in three days, Leo," he said. He picked up an oil-stiffened leather washer from his parts box and began trimming the edge with a pocketknife, turning it against his thumb to keep the bevel even. "This aquifer isn't a city pool. The bottom fifty feet is gray clay slurry. Fine silt will coat that little glass eye like grease. Your computer will think the well is dry when it's only looking at its own nose."

Leo pushed the sensor lead into the splice box, closed the cover, and wiped a muddy wrist across their forehead. "I coded a calibration offset into the module," they said. "The software accounts for a linear degradation of the optical signal. It adjusts the baseline every twenty-four hours."

"You can't code out mud, boy." Art held the washer up to the sun, checking the cut. The edge had to seat clean or the backup lever would weep under pressure. "When the sediment hits the impellers, they drift out of true a thousandth of an inch at a time. The bearings heat. The casing starts to sing. Your sensor watches light. It doesn't feel the temperature in the housing or hear the note go wrong."

He stood and laid one palm against the pump casing. The metal was warmer than it should have been for noon. Beyond the tanks, somebody in the garden shouted for more hose pressure. Somewhere on the street a hammer rang against steel. Every demand on the system arrived as sound before it arrived as data.

At dawn that morning, House 5 had reported that its upper barrel was down nearly a bucket despite no overnight draw being logged on Leo's tally sheet. Leo had blamed evaporation and the loosened lid seal from the previous storm. But Art had found a dark ribbon of damp soil running away from the buried line behind the settlement tank, narrow as a bootlace and already drying in the heat. He had pressed the mud once with the toe of his boot and said nothing. A system did not have to fail loudly to begin losing itself.

"We don't have the labor hours to run manual bucket tests every three hours, Art," Leo said. They tapped the screen of the tablet clipped to the post, and a new line graph jumped into place: *Turbidity: 4.2 NTU. Status: Nominal.* "Elena has me tracking the caloric efficiency of every gallon we lift. The model needs digital data streams to project water security through July."

Art looked down at the graph, then past it to the muddy trench where the overflow line ran. He remembered the county plant in ninety-eight after management installed bright digital flow meters over the old filter bays. The screens had been so clean the operators stopped walking the channels at night. When river weed clogged the intake during the hurricane, the sensors stayed green until the headers tore themselves off their mountings under vacuum.

"You're borrowing time from the hardware, Leo," Art said. He dropped the trimmed washer into his pocket and picked up a heavy pipe wrench from the grass. The handle was slick with old grease and grit. "Optimization without redundancy is just a loan from time. You can run a system like that for a while. Then time comes to collect in the mud."

Leo stood up, wiping their muddy knees. "The automated flush saves us four gallons of water per cycle," they said. "The script is right about the efficiency. We will calibrate the optical elements manually after the first potato harvest."

Art spat into the mud by the casing. He still did not answer. He crossed to the settlement tank and put the wrench on the packing gland of the manual backup lever, leaning his weight into it until the old brass groaned and seated. The resistance traveled back through his palms, honest and specific. That kind of feedback never lied.

Systems Panoramic

The fine silicate particles suspended in the aquifer water began to accumulate within the recessed seat of the automated solenoid valve. The microscopic grit prevented the synthetic rubber diaphragm from seating completely during the automated cleaning cycle. A silent, unmonitored backflow leakage of one point eight liters per hour began to drain from the primary storage reservoir back into the dry surface soil.

Chapter 8:
The First Harvest & The Internal Leak

Systems Panoramic

The total biomass of the cul-de-sac's converted agricultural beds reached its first measurable maturity peak. The community harvested forty-two kilograms of early-yield tubers, representing a localized caloric surge of thirty-three thousand kilocalories. The administrative database updated the regional inventory levels, shifting the community's projected resource exhaustion date by eleven days. Two hours later, a mechanical lock-state disparity occurred in the auxiliary storage bay.

Scene Core (Elena POV)

The smell of boiled potato skins and charred rosemary filled the garage, cutting through the permanent scent of damp soil and iron filings. On the workbench, a large ceramic bowl held the evening's ration, a pale, steaming mound of the first yield, still shedding curls of vapor into the light above the bench. For forty minutes, the sound of neighbors talking had a lighter, faster rhythm. People sat on the concrete floor with their backs against tool chests and the cinderblock wall, their shoulders lowered for the first time since the winter freeze, as if a body could mistake one meal for stability.

Someone had found a jar of dried rosemary in the back of a pantry. Someone else had traded three batteries for a spoonful of cooking oil. The potatoes had been halved and browned in a cast-iron pan blackened by wood smoke. They tasted of salt, ash, and almost enough. When people laughed, they did it with food still in their mouths, the quick, embarrassed laughter of a neighborhood relearning the sound.

Elena did not eat her portion. She stood by the back wall, her eyes fixed on the padlocked steel cage that held the neighborhood's medical reserves and dry grain sacks. Celebration had its own danger. It made people feel as though a problem had been solved when it had only been delayed.

Miller was laughing, his arm thrown over the back of an overturned crate, holding a steaming tuber. At the edge of the light, Henderson stood by the garage entry, his hands tucked into his tool belt, his eyes tracking the shadows along the perimeter fence outside. He didn't take a potato from the bowl.

"It's a good yield," Henderson said to the room, his voice dropping below the laughter. "But the smoke from this stove is carrying two miles down the ridge line. The folks over at the commercial corridor aren't blind. If we don't start reinforcing the southern drainage ditch with timber spikes before the root crops mature, we're just growing a garden for the first convoy that runs out of diesel."

"They're county people, Henderson," Sarah said, setting her cup down.

"They were county people when the transformers were live, Sarah," Henderson said, stepping back into the dark of the porch. "Now they're just appetites with headlamps. We watch the perimeter, or we're digging our own graves with these trowels."

The murmur from the floor grew heavier. Mrs. Albright from House 2 set her zinc plate down on her lap, the metal clinking against her belt buckle. "My husband's hands are too swollen from the weeding to hold a rifle if Henderson's convoy comes, Elena. If the script drops our ration again because his labor hours fell off, we won't have the strength to carry the timber spikes down to the ditch."

"The script isn't an executioner, Mrs. Albright," Elena said, her voice dropping into that low, flat register that quieted the room.

Elena looked at the green plastic military container behind the steel mesh cage, her eyes fixing on the stenciled lettering. For a moment she saw the white-walled corridors of the regional logistics center in Juba during the cholera spike, a terminal reporting *Zero Disparity* while children died of dehydration outside the tent flap because a decimal error had frozen the supply line. She had learned then that panic dissolved systems into scramble. She trusted the machine because it was the only thing that didn't have an accent or a family to favor.

"The model is the only reason the well hasn't run dry," Elena told the room, her hand settling onto the wire gate of the cage. "If we manage this by who has the loudest voice or the sorest hands, the street will be empty by July. We follow the printout."

The room absorbed the remark and moved on too quickly. That, more than the words themselves, bothered Elena.

She pulled her master clipboard from the wall hook. The paper sheets were gray from handling, marked with Leo's precise ink columns and her own quick checkmarks. A thumbprint of dried soil sat across the top corner of the harvest page where someone had tried to total weights before washing their hands.

"We need to log the harvest weights before the morning distribution," Leo said, walking over with the electronic tablet. The screen displayed a celebratory gold banner over the dashboard. "The model is re-calculating the baseline now. If we factor in the tuber weights, we can increase the evening caloric allocation by fifty calories per adult for the next three weeks."

The gold banner irritated Elena on sight.

"Hold the calculation, Leo," Elena said. Her voice was low, barely lifting over the noise of the neighbors laughing across the room.

She unlocked the steel cage. The padlock felt unusually cold against her fingers. She swung the heavy wire gate open and stepped into the small enclosure, her boots crunching on a few stray grains of rice that had spilled onto the floor weeks ago.

The enclosure was only six feet by eight, but it had become the nerve center of every argument on the street. One shelf held canvas sacks of grain, each stenciled by weight. One held the green plastic field case of antibiotics and trauma supplies. Leo's lock sensor and access strip sat bolted to the frame, a clean little mechanism guarding very dirty necessities.

The security seal, a thin strip of blue plastic wire she had locked through the hasp yesterday morning, was missing. In its place was a loose piece of gray utility wire, twisted into a hasty loop.

Elena stood still for one second before touching it. In that second, the room outside the cage became inventory risk.

For one misplaced heartbeat, the room beyond the mesh kept behaving like a room at supper. Someone laughed at something Miller had said. A spoon scraped the iron pan with a bright domestic sound. Then Sarah looked up and saw Elena's face. The laughter thinned without finishing. Mrs.

Albright lowered her cup. Henderson turned in the doorway, his hand dropping from his belt as if the threat had changed shape. By the time Elena touched the twisted gray wire, the garage no longer felt like a neighborhood sharing a meal. It felt like a room full of possible thieves who had just realized they were being counted.

She flipped the latches. The lid lifted with a dull pop of the rubber gasket.

"What is it?" Leo asked, stepping into the cage behind her. His tablet was still in his hand, the gold banner glowing against the dim shelves.

Elena reached inside, her hand passing over the rows of brown glass bottles. She pulled out a cardboard tray that had held their remaining supply of liquid amoxicillin, the broad-spectrum antibiotic they were conserving for deep infections.

The tray was empty. Three bottles were missing.

She dropped the tray back into the bin and moved her hand to the grain shelf behind it. A twenty-five-pound canvas sack of parboiled rice had been sliced open along the bottom seam. A clean white line of grain showed where the fabric had been evacuated into a smaller container. The cut had been made low and neat, with enough pressure to open the weave without tearing it ragged. Not panic. Intent.

"Five pounds of rice," Elena said, her eyes tracking the white line down to the dust on the lower shelf. "And the liquid amoxicillin. Someone used a knife on the seam while the garden shifts were changing this afternoon."

"The electronic lock log shows no unauthorized entry," Leo said, his fingers frantic on the tablet screen. The celebratory banner vanished as he pulled up the audit history. "The gate was only opened during the official fulfillment windows. The data says the lock state has been secure since eight AM."

"The data is wrong, Leo. Look at the floor." Elena pointed to a clear, partial boot print in the spilled flour dust beneath the grain shelf. The heel pattern was small, thin, and deep, not the heavy, square vibram tread of the work boots Art and Miller wore.

"This wasn't an outsider," Elena said. She stepped out of the cage and looked through the mesh wire at the neighbors gathered around the ceramic bowl.

Miller was still laughing. Sarah was showing a child how to whistle through a potato skin. Someone at the back of the room was scraping the cast-iron pan clean with a spoon. They looked like a neighborhood that had saved itself. Under the LED bulb, Elena felt the old, cold weight of her hospital administration years returning, the narcotics counts, the falsified signatures, the sudden understanding that desperation could wear any face in the room and still ask you for seconds.

"The lock logic didn't flag it," Leo whispered, his face turning a flat, pale color as he stared at the empty space on the shelf. "The security script didn't send an alert."

"The script only knows what the sensor tells it," Elena said, her voice dropping into the hard administrative register that left no room for negotiation. "The lock was bypassed mechanically. Someone in this room has the key, or they know how to pop the hinge pins."

She looked back at the clipboard, her pen hovering over the morning allocation column. The numbers that had looked so clean ten minutes ago were now a liability. Fifty extra calories per adult. Expanded baseline. Relaxed threshold. All of it assumed a closed loop that no longer existed.

"Cancel the fifty-calorie increase, Leo," Elena said, her face tightening as she looked back out at the room. "We don't expand the reserve floor. Tomorrow morning, we start an internal audit. We track every hour spent on the garden beds against the physical weight of what went into every kitchen, and we find out who has been carrying a knife in the dark."

Systems Panoramic

The local mesh network executed a routine status query across the twelve residential terminal nodes. Finding no anomalous voltage drops or unauthorized data access commands within the storage sector, the automated monitoring routine logged a security status code of one hundred percent compliance. The ledger file recorded the baseline as unbroken. Twenty-three meters away, five pounds of grain remained hidden beneath a loose floorboard in House 7.

PART III:
THE COLLISION ZONE

Chapter 9:
The Internal Audit

Systems Panoramic

The allocation software expanded its data schema to incorporate forty-eight behavioral metadata points. The system mapped internal transit velocity between individual residences and the agricultural core, processing tool-return latencies and baseline metabolic expenditure variances. Individuals tracking outside a standard deviation of zero point zero five were automatically prioritized for variance correction to maintain total loop stability.

Scene Core (Leo POV)

Leo's fingers left faint, greasy smudges on the plastic keys. The code on the screen was no longer a simple balance sheet. It had grown into a dense network of dependencies, an interconnected web of logic that tracked the physical movements of thirty-four people through the medium of their resource consumption.

The garage was cold enough that the metal edge of the keyboard tray bit into Leo's wrists. A thin smell of wet soil drifted in through the cracked side window, mixed with printer ozone, old solder, and the faint medicinal vinegar rising from the sterilized sheets drying next door. On the pegboard above the monitor, garden twine, hose clamps, and a spare brass float valve hung in neat rows. The order of the tools made the scatter plots on the screen feel cleaner than they were.

Leo dragged the stylus across the trackpad and opened the revised audit module. New windows tiled themselves across the display: labor logs, household weights, gate-sensor transit stamps, tool-return times, ration withdrawals, and the running caloric baseline for the twelve houses. Each pane pulsed in a slightly different shade of green as the code pulled yesterday's entries from the local cache and stripped them into comparable units. Seconds. Pounds. Calories. Distance walked. Output per hour. What had been lived in argument and muscle was being rendered into variance.

Outside, the eight o'clock watering queue had already formed by the gate. Leo could hear bucket handles striking one another and the flat impatient murmur of neighbors who had not yet seen the revised allocations but already knew something in the system had tightened.

The line outside the gate had acquired the habits of an office no one had wanted to build. Buckets were set in rank order on the gravel to mark place. People compared yesterday's slips in low, clipped voices, pointing at decimal differences as if they were clauses in a contract. When one boy from House 11 tried to step ahead to ask whether his mother's fever counted as a protected variance, Henderson told him to get back in sequence because the audit would process every household in turn. The waiting itself had become part of the routine now, another choreographed scarcity that made everyone sound more official than humane.

"The model is identifying the anomaly," Leo said, not turning around as the garage door creaked.

Elena stepped into the room, carrying a stack of handwritten labor logs from the garden shifts. The pages were soft at the corners from sweat and repeated handling. Her face was gray in the morning twilight, and there was dried mud on the hem of her work pants. "The neighbors are waiting at the gate, Leo. Miller is refusing to start the morning watering until he gets his full ration. He says the audit is treating everyone like prisoners."

Leo held out a hand without looking. Elena slapped the logs against the desk, and Leo flattened them beside the keyboard, weighting the top page with a rusted socket wrench so the damp paper would stop curling. The pencil columns were familiar now: names, hours, crop row, assigned task, carried weight, injury status. Human labor translated into a ledger narrow enough to fit a machine.

"The audit is tracking probability, not people," Leo said, pointing the stylus at a series of clustered scatter plots on the monitor. "I cross-referenced the physical calorie consumption of each household against their agricultural output over the past fourteen days. Look at House 7. The Davis family."

Elena leaned over the back of the chair, her breath catching. Her shadow crossed the display, dimming one corner of the graph. "They have been hitting their planting quotas every day."

Leo tapped twice and expanded the household panel. A row of figures dropped open beneath the Davis name: daily intake, labor output, body-weight entries, gate scans, and the exact intervals between House 7 and the storage bay across fourteen days. Leo had written the subroutine after midnight, adding a correction factor for work performed on broken roadbed and a second one for water hauling on the north slope. The code had accepted both adjustments without argument. It had accepted everything.

"They have been hitting their quotas, but their biological efficiency metric is mathematically impossible," Leo said. "The model calculates that Mrs. Davis should have lost one point two kilograms of body mass based on the caloric value of the food she was allocated versus the physical foot-pounds of energy she expended breaking base stone on Tuesday. But her manual weight log shows her mass is completely stable."

Elena reached past Leo and steadied herself on the edge of the desk. Her thumbnail was split down the middle, packed dark with soil. "She could have a slower metabolism, Leo. The model cannot account for individual genetics."

Leo hit the recalculate key. The processor bar flickered, then ran the same conclusion back at them in the same indifferent tone. "The variance is too large for genetics, Elena. The script ran a simulation across five thousand baseline iterations. The probability of her maintaining that specific mass without an external caloric input is less than zero point zero two percent. They have an unlogged food source."

He opened the gate log and dragged the time cursor across Thursday afternoon. The garage printer clicked once as if clearing its throat. On the monitor, a blue transit line lifted away from the garden cluster and crossed toward the storage cage. Leo zoomed in until the timestamps separated into individual minutes. A second pane populated with lock-state history, hinge movement, and the fulfillment windows Elena had authorized by hand. The machine was no longer counting food. It was tracking deviation.

He hit the enter key. The script isolated a specific time window on the tracking matrix: *Thursday, 14:15 to 14:45.*

"During the afternoon shift change," Leo continued, "the sensor on the garden gate registered that Eli Davis left the plot fifteen minutes before his replacement arrived. The auxiliary storage cage is exactly sixty meters from that path. The model matches the time deficit perfectly with the missing amoxicillin and the five pounds of rice."

Elena was silent for several seconds. Outside, a bucket struck concrete somewhere up the lane. Through the small garage window, House 7 was visible between two bare lilac bushes, a thin plume of woodsmoke rising from the chimney in a straight gray line.

"Mrs. Davis's oldest child has a chronic ear infection," Elena said, her voice dropping into a flat, hollow tone. "The fluid behind the eardrum hasn't cleared since February. She came to the clinic porch last week asking if we had any pediatric drops left. I told her the amoxicillin was reserved for systemic trauma."

Leo looked back at the screen. The Davis row remained highlighted in pale green, as neat and regular as a measured cut of copper pipe. On the shelf beside the monitor sat the sealed plastic bin that held replacement keyboard parts, sorted by size and function. On the floor beneath it was a crate of split hickory for Art's stove. Both systems made sense when they stayed in their own containers.

"The model doesn't look at the ear infection, Elena," Leo said. Their hands felt cold against the keyboard. "The model looks at the theft. If we let five pounds of grain and three bottles of medicine vanish without an adjustment, the baseline calculation for the entire cul-de-sac drops below the safety margin by July tenth. Everything fails because of the leak."

Elena reached out, her finger hovering over the confirmation key on the keyboard. Her hand did not shake, but the muscle beneath her ear twitched once, hard enough to show in the gray light. Outside, one of the waiting neighbors knocked hard on the garage door frame and called for the numbers. Elena did not answer.

"Apply the variance penalty," Elena said.

Leo did not hit the key immediately. He reopened the Davis panel, checked the labor rows a second time, then verified the household count against the census file. Thirty-four residents. Three hundred and forty-two thousand kilocalories before correction. Safety margin projected to fail by July tenth if the leak remained unaddressed. The code returned the same conclusion each time. There was comfort in that. Machines did not ask whether you wanted to remain decent. They only returned thresholds.

Leo pressed execute.

The script automatically recalculated the allocation matrix for House 7. The display updated instantly: *Household 7: Caloric Allocation Reduced by 35% for 14 Days. Medical Access Status: Suspended.*

A relay clicked in the storage-bay control box on the far wall. The small receipt printer on the shelf woke with a dry mechanical chatter and began feeding out the revised ration slip in narrow increments, each line of ink arriving with the same crisp finality as a gate latch dropping into place. Leo watched the paper advance past the cutter blade. The machine had no hesitation built into it.

The printer finished its cycle, dropping the slip into the tray. Leo picked it up to hand to Elena, but the garage door didn't just creak, it stayed open.

Twelve-year-old Toby Davis was standing on the gravel outside, holding an empty tin lard bucket by the wire handle. His face was smudged with soot from his family's stove, his breathing shallow enough that the collar of his oversized flannel shirt rattled against his collarbone. He looked at the glowing screen, then down at the small slip of paper in Leo's hand.

Water dripped from the hem of the boy's pants onto the threshold. One bootlace was broken and retied in a hard knot around the ankle. The lard bucket was clean inside, scrubbed bright from repeated use, and light enough that it swung when his hand trembled.

"My mom said the box didn't clear the balance," the boy said. He didn't come inside. He stayed on the wet gravel, his boots dripping mud onto the doorsill. "She said the light on the gate turned red when she scanned the handle."

Leo looked from the boy's thin wrists to the screen, where *Household 7: Caloric Allocation Reduced by 35%* remained solid green. The code didn't have a font size for the wire handle vibrating in the boy's hand.

Elena did not step forward. She stood with one hand braced on the desk, her eyes fixed on the ration slip as if reading it again might change the arithmetic. Outside, the waiting line had gone quiet enough for Leo to hear the light clink of another bucket being set down in the dirt.

"The allocation adjusted this morning," Leo said. The words felt heavy, like dry sand in the mouth. "The balance shifted."

The boy didn't argue. He looked at the paper one more time, set the empty lard bucket down on the porch stone, and turned back toward House 7, his shoulder blades shifting sharply under the thin wool of his coat.

Leo listened to the bucket handle settle against the metal rim with a small, bright tap after the boy let go of it. Then the yard went quiet again except for the low electrical hum of the monitor and the distant clank of the watering gate where the neighbors were still waiting for a number to tell them what to do.

Then, from outside, someone in the waiting line cleared a throat and asked whether House 4's water allotment had been adjusted yet. The question was quiet, almost embarrassed, but it broke the spell more completely than shouting would have. A bucket handle clicked against concrete. Another household shifted forward half a step toward the porch without looking at the road Toby had taken. The morning queue resumed its shape around the absence he left behind, and Leo felt, with a sickness deeper than guilt, how quickly a regime could teach decent people to continue.

Systems Panoramic

The allocation script on the master garage node processed forty-two data updates following the baseline correction. Total calorie values stabilized at three hundred and thirty-seven thousand kilocalories. The correction registered as successful, entering a low-power monitoring cycle until the scheduled eight point zero zero automated ledger synchronization.

Chapter 10:
The Dust at the Gate

Systems Panoramic

The asphalt surface of Silverbrook Road registered a sustained seismic vibration of forty-two hertz. The thermal sensors on the perimeter of Sub-District 4-A recorded a rapid increase in infrared signatures as six internal combustion engines dropped their speed to ten kilometers per hour. The local atmospheric dust density rose by twelve milligrams per cubic meter along the southern approach to the cul-de-sac.

Scene Core (Art POV)

Art saw the dust before he heard the engines. He was standing on his front porch, cleaning the threads of an old brass gate valve with a wire brush. The gray cloud rose above the pine line at the intersection of Silverbrook, thick and dry, the sign of heavy vehicles moving fast on a road that hadn't seen a maintenance truck in a year.

He stopped brushing. The brass part sat in his palm with its threads half-cleaned, the old grease loosened but not wiped away. Below the dust plume, sunlight flashed once on a windshield, then vanished. Too many vehicles. Too much weight on the road. Not county service, not anymore.

Art dropped the valve into his canvas pocket, took the porch steps two at a time, and walked down to the perimeter gate.

Elena was already there, her hand resting on the padlocked iron chain that linked the two sections of the security fence. Miller stood beside her, holding a five-foot piece of galvanized pipe like a club. Henderson was farther back by the ditch, checking the timber spikes they had driven into the runoff trench after the harvest dinner. Nobody spoke. Even the children on the porches had gone quiet. The cul-de-sac had gone still in the way a body goes still before impact.

Six vehicles, four outdated commercial delivery vans and two rusted station wagons, came around the bend and ground to a halt twenty feet from the iron line. Their suspensions sagged under load. One rear tire was wrapped with a strip of baling wire where the steel belt had begun to separate. Another van had a cracked headlamp patched with clear packing tape gone brown at the edges. The tailpipes sputtered, spitting gray clouds of unburnt diesel into the humid spring air.

The doors didn't open immediately. For two minutes the vehicles sat idling, a row of dented metal hulls covered in road grime and pale handprints. The engines knocked unevenly, some cylinders missing on the low end. Through the dirty side glass Art could make out shapes packed shoulder to shoulder, the stillness of people conserving calories even while the machine beneath them shook. Condensation fogged one rear window from the inside, then cleared with the slow swipe of a sleeve.

A child coughed inside the second van. The sound was muffled by the bodywork but carried cleanly across the gap. Behind Art, Miller shifted his grip higher on the pipe.

Behind Art, the cul-de-sac registered the convoy before anyone had words for it. A curtain on the Albrights' front window twitched twice and held. One of Miller's boys stepped barefoot onto the porch despite the gravel heat and was pulled back by the collar before he could wave. From somewhere up the lane came the smell of hot coolant and bad brakes before the people themselves were fully visible. Henderson had already shifted his stance toward the ditch line, not speaking, just measuring how much road remained between the lead bumper and the gate.

Then the driver's side door of the lead van groaned open.

A man climbed out. He wore a stained reflective vest over a heavy winter coat, his trousers stiff with dried mud at the cuffs. He walked with a pronounced limp, his left hand holding a plastic clipboard against his chest. His face was hollow, covered in a week of gray stubble, but Art recognized the way the man held his head, the stiff bureaucratic posture of a man who had spent thirty years writing municipal engineering specifications and signing off on cost-saving compromises he knew were bad steel dressed up as policy.

"Marcus," Art said, his voice scratching in his throat.

Dr. Marcus Calder stopped five feet from the gate. He looked through the iron bars at Art, his bloodshot eyes blinking slowly against the glare of the sun. He did not smile. He raised the plastic clipboard, pointing the metal clip toward the cul-de-sac behind Art.

"The water plant at the reservoir went dry on Tuesday, Art," Marcus said. His voice was thin, raspy from dust. "The automated intake valves jammed with silt from the low pool, and the computer locked the control room from the Richmond hub. We couldn't bypass the software without the administrator's encryption key, and the state office has been empty since April."

He took one folded sheet off the clipboard and held it through the bars. The page was a plant emergency log, damp and oil-marked, covered in hurried signatures and pressure readings written by hand after the terminals had gone dark. Art did not take it. He could see enough from where he stood: suction loss, intake cavitation, operator override denied. The handwriting changed twice down the page. Shift handoff in a crisis.

"I told you the software was a trap back in eighteen, Marcus," Art said, his fingers tightening around the cold iron bar of the gate. "I told you if you didn't keep the manual overrides on the hydraulic lines, you were building a tomb."

"You were right about the overrides. You were right about everything," Marcus said. The words came out without heat, worn down by lack of water and the long distance between being right and being useful. He looked past Art toward the green potato patches growing in the old roadway. "We have twenty-six people in the vans. Four of them are former operators from the treatment facility. Three are children from the county health office. We have two gallons of chlorinated pool water left in the plastic drums, and the children have been purging since yesterday from the sediment."

As if to confirm it, the side door of the second van slid open six inches from the inside and stuck. A small arm appeared in the gap, then withdrew. The smell reached the gate a second later: diesel, old vomit, wet cloth, and the mineral stink of bad water sitting in warm plastic. Someone inside retched weakly.

Elena stepped up beside Art, her master clipboard tucked under her arm. Her eyes moved first to the passengers, then to the cargo weight on the axles, then to the rusting roof racks tied down with extension cord. Art knew that look. She was already counting liters, bodies, work-hours, and spoilage loss.

"We have a closed resource loop here," Elena said, her voice dropping into her flat, operational register. "Our acreage is calculated down to the square foot for twelve households. We don't have the baseline capacity to support twenty-six extra mouths."

Marcus looked at Elena, his gaze fixing on her hospital name tag, which was still pinned to her coat. "I know you, Elena," he said. "I signed the emergency water variance for your dialysis wing during the summer freeze three years ago. I kept your line live when the city was cutting the commercial sectors. We ran the risk for your facility."

Elena did not look away, but Art saw her chin drop a fraction of an inch. The spreadsheet logic she had used to run the morning census was colliding directly with the ghost of her own institutional past.

"Things are different now, Marcus," Elena said. "We don't run on variances."

Art looked past them at the lead van. A small face, a girl no older than Leo's age when the blackouts started, was pressing her forehead against the passenger glass. Her skin had the pale, waxy color of someone running out of fluid. Another passenger sat behind her with a rag tied across the lower half of the face like a failed dust mask. On the rear seat of the station wagon, a pair of work boots hung upside down by their laces, drying over a cracked heater vent that no longer mattered.

Art reached into his pocket and felt the hard, specific weight of his leather notebook. Marcus was the man who had filed the paperwork that had forced Art out of the authority, the man who had chosen the clean, automated corporate contracts over Art's analog redundancies. But Marcus was also the only living person left who knew the exact diameter of the primary conduit under Silverbrook Road, the only one who remembered how to balance a water main by the sound of the flow.

"They have four operators, Elena," Art said, turning his head to look at his daughter. "They aren't just mouths. They are hands. If the well bearings seize next week, Leo can't fix them with a line of code. We need people who know how to pour babbitt. We need people who have opened a live housing under pressure."

"And if we open the gate for twenty-six, what do I tell Miller's family when the July reserve collapses?" Elena asked. She still had one hand on the chain. "What do I tell Tommy when the antibiotic reserve is gone because we treated a convoy instead of the fracture we already own?"

No one answered her. The vans idled. A thin ribbon of steam lifted from one cracked radiator seam. Marcus shifted his bad leg and nearly lost balance before catching himself on the gate. Henderson looked down the road once, toward the commercial corridor, as if checking whether more engines might be coming behind these.

"The algorithm handles the capacity, Art," Elena said at last, her hand still resting on the padlock. "We don't make the calculation at the gate. We plug the metrics into the system first."

Systems Panoramic

The automated allocation model inside Leo's garage registered a twenty-four percent data latency alert as the local mesh network processed the presence of sixty-two unauthorized mobile devices at the southern perimeter. The script remained in monitoring state, waiting for a manual text string input to recalculate the community's carrying capacity.

Chapter 11:
The Triage Algorithm

Systems Panoramic

The regional procurement registry completed its daily synchronization sequence. The sector classification database updated the entry for Sub-District 4-A from *Active Residential Zone* to *Unmonitored Sector - Zero Priority*. The twenty-two non-selected individual profiles associated with the incoming manifest were flagged as *Extraneous Static Variances* and scrubbed from the active memory sectors to optimize storage overhead. The administrative network achieved a state of absolute data efficiency.

Scene Core (Elena POV)

Elena clicked the mouse, her eyes scanning the raw rows of text Leo had transcribed from Marcus's plastic clipboard. The garage was entirely silent, save for the rhythmic clicking of the cooling fan on the battery bank behind her and the faint metallic tick of rainwater dripping from somebody's coat onto the concrete by the door.

The overhead work light cast a hard white circle across the bench. Inside it lay the convoy manifest, copied by hand onto lined paper from Marcus's damp municipal forms. The pages had already begun to curl where the rain had dried unevenly. Each entry had been broken into the fields Leo's model required: age, sex, injury status, disease burden, labor history, mechanical skill, current caloric condition. Elena had spent years moving human beings through hospital intake systems, but the neatness of the columns still made her shoulders feel cold.

Marcus Calder. Fifty-eight years old. Chronic venous insufficiency in the lower left limb, reducing physical labor capacity by forty percent.

Below his line were the others. Three children with active gastrointestinal symptoms. A mechanic with a crushed thumb healing crooked. Two plant operators with moderate dehydration and one with a persistent cough. Jared Turner, age twenty-four, lean enough that the body-mass estimate had to be guessed from a wet jacket and a standing silhouette at the gate. Kara Calder, age twenty-two, mechanical competence noted twice in Marcus's hand. Ruiz, R., age twenty-seven, agricultural labor. Mason, M., age nineteen, salvage electrical. The list tried to make the human load look sortable.

Elena moved the cursor down the page one name at a time, checking each field against the hand-written notes clipped to the side of the monitor. The paper smelled faintly of wet cardboard, diesel, and the stale sourness of bodies that had ridden too long in closed vehicles. Through the garage wall she could hear the low churn of the cul-de-sac outside, not conversation exactly, but the held-back murmur of people waiting for a decision to come out of a room they were not in.

Leo stood over her shoulder with one finger touching the glass. The reflected green data bars moved across their face each time the interface refreshed. "The medical metrics are dragging the curve down," Leo said. "If we factor in the three children with the water-borne infection, the model drops our potato reserve safety margin below thirty days. It automatically flags the intake as a critical failure."

Elena clicked into the pediatric rows and opened the treatment assumptions tab. Small boxes appeared for antibiotics, fluid replacement, isolation labor, and projected recovery time. She had helped build hospital dashboards like this before the retreat, tools that pretended uncertainty could be reduced to a stable menu of options. She hated how familiar the interface felt under her hand.

"What if we exclude the children from the medical priority queue?" Elena asked. Her fingers remained flat on the edge of the desk, frozen there as if stillness could keep the decision from becoming real. "If we treat them with local herbal charcoal instead of the amoxicillin, does the baseline recover?"

Leo leaned in and ran the alternative. The processor icon turned twice, then a fresh set of numbers populated the graph. A yellow warning triangle appeared in the lower right corner and stayed there. "It recovers by four days," Leo said, his voice flat, devoid of inflection. "But the survival probability for those three nodes drops to forty-five percent. The algorithm recalculates their labor contribution to zero for the next six months. It doesn't balance, Elena."

She stared at the triangle until the color began to feel like an accusation. Outside, a hand struck the hood of a vehicle once, then stopped. Somebody coughed near the gate. Somebody else called for a bucket. The neighborhood was already behaving as if the answer had mass, as if it would have to be lifted and carried by somebody before nightfall.

Elena closed her eyes for three seconds. She remembered the emergency room intake logs from her second year at the hospital network, when a multi-car pileup on Interstate 95 had brought seventeen red-tagged traumas into a facility with four open bays. She had spent two hours behind a glass window, matching names to color-coded plastic bracelets based on a standardized triage card. The card had removed her name from the choice. The card was the authority. Families screamed at the glass, and she only had to point at color.

She opened her eyes and reached for Marcus's line again. The pointer hovered over his labor coefficient. Forty percent deficit. Reduced mobility. High skill value, low immediate output. The machine had no field for debt owed, history kept, or the sound of a man who knew where the buried flush valves lay under county soil. It had no field for the summer freeze, for the water variance he had once signed to keep her patients alive. It had no field for gratitude.

Outside the garage, the cul-de-sac was quiet in the strained way a waiting room is quiet. A porch step creaked. The chain at the southern gate rattled once in the wind. The whole neighborhood was waiting for the screen to choose its acceptable dead.

"Run the carrying-capacity model with operator-weighted skill retention," Elena said.

Leo changed the weighting field. Mechanical competence rose. Pediatric burden remained red. Projected drawdown widened, then narrowed, then failed again. The graph bent upward for six seconds and collapsed below threshold.

"And with minimum pediatric support?" Elena asked.

Leo ran it. "Still unstable."

"And with full quarantine labor counted against us?"

Leo did not answer immediately. He hit enter, watched the output settle, and then said, "Critical failure in twenty-one days."

The garage seemed smaller after that. The monitor fan clicked. The receipt printer on the shelf gave a tiny preparatory stir as if it could sense a command before one was issued. Elena could feel the pressure gathering in the room around the simple fact that every alternative still ended with her having to say no to someone by name.

She hit the function key to run the final resource integration sequence.

The screen flickered twice as the processor loaded the carrying capacity matrix. A single vertical status bar grew from the left edge of the interface, moving from amber to a pale, solid gray. On the shelf beside the bench, the receipt printer woke with a soft mechanical stir before any result had even appeared, as if the hardware already trusted the outcome.

The text generated on the screen was clear:

RE-ALLOCATION SUMMARY: MATRIX UPDATED

Maximum Integration Limit to Maintain Current Baseline: 4 Nodes.

RECOMMENDED INTRA-SYSTEM SELECTION:

1. Node 35: Turner, J. (Age 24) — High Caloric-to-Labor Efficiency.
2. Node 36: Calder, K. (Age 22) — Mechanical Competence / Filter Tech.
3. Node 37: Ruiz, R. (Age 27) — Agricultural Labor Asset.
4. Node 38: Mason, M. (Age 19) — Electrical Salvage Competence.

Warning: Integration of Node 39 (Calder, M.) or remaining twenty-one unlisted nodes exceeds sector carrying capacity. System collapse projected for June 14.

Elena stared at the name *Calder, M.* on the screen. The software had rejected Marcus. It had looked at his forty-percent physical deficit and his fifty-eight years of age and had categorized him as a waste product in the balance sheet of the cul-de-sac.

"It selected the four youngest operators," Leo whispered, their fingers twitching against the rubber frame of the tablet. "The ones who can work twelve-hour shifts on the asphalt beds immediately. It left the families."

Elena reached over and took the printed receipt when it emerged, warm and smooth from the cutter. The paper was clean, white, and perfectly balanced between what the model called viable and what it had already discarded. Holding it, she felt the old relief again, the same administrative numbness the triage card had once provided. The answer sat outside her now. That was the seduction.

The relief shamed her almost as soon as she felt it. For one stripped second, the recommendation on the paper seemed to spare her from becoming the person who chose which child stayed in the rain and which one crossed the line. But that was the corruption in its cleanest form. The machine had not removed her from the decision. It had only translated her willingness to abandon them into a format tidy enough to hold.

"The model is doing what we built it to do, Leo," she said. Her voice sounded thin, like dry paper scraping against stone. "It is protecting what is left. If we override the recommendation and let all twenty-six in, we aren't saving them. We are just choosing to starve with them three weeks earlier."

She stood up, her keycard lanyard rattling against the zipper of her coat. The list remained in her hand, warm for only a second before the garage air turned it cold.

"Let's go to the gate," Elena said. "We have to deliver the allocation."

Systems Panoramic

The auxiliary storage cage relays adjusted their access logs to prepare for the addition of four new resource accounts. The internal system clocks synchronized to the millisecond, ready to meter out the extra four hundred and fifty calories per day at the morning gate census. The database maintained its solid green status icon, tracking the adjustment as a localized technical optimization.

Chapter 12:
The Three-Way Floor Debate

Systems Panoramic

The local mesh network processed a three hundred percent increase in internal message traffic between the residential terminals. The data packets contained unencrypted string variations of the words *ration, gate, safety*, and *inventory*. The distribution server queued these communications, prioritizing the system's baseline status reports over the high-frequency emotional variance of the user interactions.

Scene Core (Leo POV)

Leo kept their hands buried inside their sweatshirt pockets to hide the shaking. The living room of House 1 was packed so tight the air had turned thick and humid, fogging the lower panes of the bay window. Thirty people sat shoulder to shoulder on floor cushions, folding chairs, and overturned crates. Wet coats hung from chair backs, giving off the smell of damp wool, clay, woodsmoke, and the faint medicinal sweetness of salve rubbed into cracked hands after ditch work.

The room had been arranged for order and was already failing to hold it. Elena's clipboard lay open on the coffee table beside a box of sharpened pencils, the evening ration ledger, and a ceramic mug half full of cold tea nobody had touched. A lantern on the mantel threw a hard yellow light over the center of the rug, leaving the edges of the room in shadow. Every time someone shifted, knees knocked chair legs or a boot scraped over the bare floorboards. The house itself seemed too small for the decision it was being asked to contain.

In the center of the rug sat the small plastic printer, its paper tongue hanging out with the names of the four approved refugees. Leo could hear the soft cooling ticks from its housing as if the thing were still finishing the choice. Beside it, the tablet screen cast a flat blue rectangle across Leo's knees, the carrying-capacity curve holding its clean downward slope with intolerable calm.

"The model is not a political opinion," Leo said, looking down at the screen to avoid the eyes of the neighbors. The tablet felt heavier than it had that morning. "It is a reflection of our physical inventory. If we integrate Marcus and the families, the daily drawdown on the well accelerates past our filtration capacity. The sand beds will saturate with silt by mid-June."

Somebody near the hallway muttered. A child asked a question and was hushed. A chair leg thumped once against the wall. Leo did not look up. The graph on the tablet remained clean, the projected line dropping exactly where it had dropped in the garage.

"Marcus Calder kept the medical line alive for this county when you were still in middle school, Leo," Art said. He was standing by the cold fireplace, his arms crossed over his chest, his gaze cutting straight through the blue light of the screen. "He isn't a node. He's the engineer who mapped the very line we are drinking from. You are letting a screen tell us that his life is worth less than four hundred calories of seed potato."

A murmur moved through the room at Marcus's name. Mrs. Davis shifted her youngest child higher on her lap. Henderson remained standing by the doorframe with both hands resting on his belt, as if he had been posted there to monitor not the discussion but the perimeter of the house itself.

"It isn't just about Marcus, Art," Elena said, stepping between Leo and her father. Her voice was flat, hard, and steady, the same voice she used when an emergency room floor was overcrowded and somebody still needed the room to sound organized. "If we override the calculation for Marcus because we know him, what do we say to the other twenty-two people in those vans? Do we look the mothers in the eye and tell them their children can't stay because they didn't work for the county water authority? The model gives us a neutral, fair standard. It removes our personal sentiment from the safety of the group."

"Fair to who?" Miller shouted from the back row, rising so fast his folding chair snapped shut behind his knees. His face had gone red under the sunburn, and the bandage at the base of his thumb showed through the gap in his glove. He pointed toward the window with the hand that wasn't injured. "My family took a thirty-five percent ration cut this week because your script decided we didn't break enough rock on Tuesday. Now you want to bring in four young strangers just because they have high labor ratings? They don't belong to this street. They didn't freeze with us in December."

The room tightened around his words. Sarah started to answer, then stopped when Miller's chair toppled fully onto its side with a hard crack. Someone near the back swore under his breath. Leo watched the printer slip stir in the draft from the back hall. The names on it looked less like admissions now than like a list of things about to be contested physically.

Henderson stepped forward before Elena could regain the room. He did not look at Art, and he did not look at the tablet. He looked at the front windows, then at the shut door, then back at Elena, measuring exits and weak points the way other people measured arguments.

"Miller is right, but for the wrong reasons," Henderson said, his voice dropping into a low, gravelly register that quieted the room more effectively than shouting. "The model says we can take four people. I say the model is being too generous. We shouldn't let *any* of them in."

Leo blinked, looking up from the data logs. "The model confirms we can sustain four nodes without dropping below the safety margin, Henderson. The carrying capacity allows for it."

"The capacity allows for it on paper, kid," Henderson said, turning to face Leo at last. He jabbed one finger toward the printer slip on the rug but did not touch it. "But what happens when those four people realize we turned their families away? They'll be working our garden beds while their brothers and children are starving outside our fence. How long before one of them pops the lock on the tool shed or opens the gate in the middle of the night? If we take those four, we are bringing twenty-six enemies inside our perimeter. We lock the gate permanently. No entries. No exceptions."

"You don't know them," Sarah said from the wall, but her voice was partly swallowed by the noise already beginning to rise around her.

"And you do?" somebody shot back from the kitchen doorway.

As the voices climbed, the room began sorting itself before anyone admitted that was what was happening. Art's supporters drifted toward the cold fireplace and the hallway leading to the kitchen, making space near the back door as if solidarity required room to move. Henderson's sympathizers gathered nearer the front windows and the entryway, shoulders angled toward the street, every posture implying perimeter first. The households who still looked to Elena remained around the coffee table and the lantern, close to the clipboard, close to the paper, as if legitimacy might still be located in the objects at the center of the rug. Leo saw Mrs. Davis notice the divisions and pull her child tighter into her lap, not choosing a side so much as trying not to be crushed between them.

The room fractured into a wall of sound. Miller was nodding, shouting across the rug at Art. Mrs. Davis was crying quietly by the door, one hand resting on the pocket where her reduced ration receipt was tucked. A man near the radiator demanded to see the numbers. A woman on the stairs asked who exactly had authorized Leo's script in the first place. The lantern flame jumped as the air shifted with the movement of bodies. Someone kicked the fallen chair aside and it skidded into the baseboard with a flat wooden slap.

Elena reached for the clipboard and slapped it flat against the coffee table. The crack got them two seconds of silence.

"Enough," she said.

For a moment, the room held. Art had moved one step off the hearth, his jaw set, his hands open at his sides as if he were trying not to close them into fists. Leo could hear their own pulse in the sleeve of the sweatshirt.

Then Miller spoke over her. Henderson answered him. Sarah tried to cut in. The noise surged back, larger than before.

Leo looked down at the screen again. The network was stable. The metrics were precise. The carrying-capacity line still held. But the three positions in the room were tearing the social fabric of the cul-de-sac apart in real time. Art wanted solidarity based on memory. Elena wanted managed triage based on data. Henderson wanted an absolute border based on fear. The code had organized the problem so cleanly that everyone could now point to it.

Systems Panoramic

The allocation script on the master node registered a manual override attempt from Terminal 9, as Henderson's home terminal requested a permanent lock-state change for the southern perimeter gate. The central script denied the request, citing a priority conflict with the master administrative profile held in Leo's garage. The mechanical locks remained in their provisional queue, waiting for a single, unified command string.

Chapter 13:
The Amputation

Systems Panoramic

The outdoor ambient light level at the southern perimeter of Sub-District 4-A decreased to less than five lumens per square meter. At nineteen point forty-five hours, the automated physical access system logged the transition of four identity accounts from *Pending* to *Resident.* The status fields for the remaining twenty-two individuals associated with the convoy transport manifest were deleted from the local network memory cache, completing the allocation adjustment.

Scene Core (Art POV)

Art held the cold iron beam of the gate with both hands, his weight pressed against the frame to keep it from swinging wide in the evening wind. The metal had already pulled the heat out of his palms. A single battery-powered floodlight had been wired to the fence post above his shoulder, and its yellow beam cut across the roadbed in a hard cone, illuminating the small circle of gravel where the choice was being carried out.

Beyond the light, the convoy sat in darkness. The van engines were off now. Without the vibration of the idling motors, the night felt too still. Art could hear the thin ticking of hot engine blocks cooling, the hiss of wind moving through the pines, and somewhere inside one of the cargo bays, a child coughing in short, wet bursts.

Elena stood three feet to his left. She held the printed sheet of paper in her gloved hand, the edge of it lifting slightly each time the wind came down the hill. Her voice carried through the dark like a rhythmic, mechanical signal.

"Node Thirty-Five," she called out. "Jared Turner. Step forward."

For a second nobody moved. Then a young man with a canvas backpack left the shadow of the lead delivery van. He did not look back at the grease-stained windows. He walked toward the gate with his chin down, his boots scraping through the grit in slow, measured strokes. Henderson stood on the inside of the fence, one hand resting on the heavy padlock chain, letting the boy pass through a narrow twelve-inch gap before snapping the iron links tight again. The sound of the chain closing was small, but it carried.

Art could feel the people behind him listening to each closure as if it were a count.

"Node Thirty-Six. Kara Calder."

Art watched his younger second cousin, Marcus's daughter, step into the floodlight. She had her father's wide, deep-set eyes, but her lips were white, trembling as she pressed her fingers once against Marcus's shoulder before moving toward the iron bars. Marcus did not reach for her. He stood flat-footed in the dust, his plastic clipboard hanging loose by his side, his lower left leg swollen against the torn seam of his trousers.

When Henderson opened the gap for her, Art saw her mouth move. He could not hear the words. The floodlight had washed her face so pale that the wet tracks on her cheeks looked like scratches in glass.

Elena kept reading. The paper did not shake in her hand.

By the time the third approved name crossed the line, the geometry of the scene had changed. Four chosen bodies were now on the inside shoulder of the road, standing in an awkward row with their bags at their feet, not speaking to the people they had left behind and not looking at the people who had admitted them. The space between inside and outside had gone from theoretical to measured.

"Node Thirty-Eight. Mason, M."

A boy with a narrow chest and a torn wool cap came out of the dark beside the second van. He could not have been more than nineteen. He hesitated once when he reached Marcus's shoulder, then stepped past him without touching him. Behind the van glass, shapes moved but did not emerge. Art saw one open hand lift to the window and flatten there, then withdraw.

The chain opened and closed again.

Marcus shifted his weight forward on his good leg. His voice, when it came, dropped below the hiss of the wind through the pines. "Art. The boy from the health office isn't going to make the night if he stays in the cargo bay. The air is stagnant in there. Just take the child. Put him under the workbench in the cellar. I won't ask for a grain of the rice."

Art looked through the iron mesh. The child was visible now, huddled in the open side door of the second van, his small frame shaking under a dirty wool blanket. The blanket rose and fell too fast. One bare ankle showed beneath it, thin as split kindling.

Art reached into his pocket and felt the hard, specific weight of his leather notebook. His fingers traced the raised ridge of the spine. He could override Elena right now. He could let go of the gate, lift the heavy wrench from his belt, strike the padlock from Henderson's hand, and force the iron frame open. He still had the shoulder strength for one clean blow.

But he looked past Marcus at the five separate households standing along the edge of the asphalt behind him. Miller was watching his own son on the inside of the fence, his jaw set in a hard, protective line. Henderson had his shoulder jammed against the gatepost, his eyes fixed not on Marcus but on the dark wood line across the road, already braced for what he thought would come next. Sarah stood ten feet back with both hands over her mouth. If Art broke the lock, the cul-de-sac would split into a physical brawl before the vans could even clear the ditch. The optimization script hadn't created the scarcity. It had only given their terror a clinical name.

Marcus waited. The wind lifted the edge of his reflective vest and let it fall again.

"I can't do it, Marcus," Art said. The words tasted like lead in his mouth.

Marcus did not flinch. He looked at Elena first, then at Leo, who stood ten feet back in the shadow of the garage wall, holding the rubber-cased tablet against their ribs like a shield. "You're letting the boy's numbers write the law, Art," Marcus said. He did not raise his voice. "You think because the machine doesn't have a heart, your hands stay clean when you turn the key. But you're the ones turning it."

Nobody answered him. The floodlight hummed. Somewhere behind Art, one of the admitted four set a bag down on the ground, then picked it up again.

"The selection is complete," Elena said. Her voice did not rise, but she folded the printed paper slip in half and tucked it into her pocket. "The gate is locked for the evening shift. Move your vehicles twenty meters back from the perimeter line, Marcus. The security sensors will flag any vehicle within the buffer zone as a threat."

Marcus looked at Art for five seconds. The muscles in his jaw moved once. Then he turned around, his bad leg dragging through the gravel, and climbed back into the driver's seat of the lead van.

The starter motor cranked three times, a hollow metallic scream in the quiet, before the diesel engine caught. One by one the remaining vans shifted into reverse. Their headlights swept across the front faces of the cul-de-sac houses, throwing long, skeletal shadows across the cabbage patches in the roadbed and across the four chosen figures now standing inside the perimeter. For an instant the beam caught the child in the cargo bay again, blanket pulled tight to his throat. Then the light slid away.

The convoy backed down the hill in stages, stopping once when the rear tires of the second van dropped into the shoulder rut, then pulling free and continuing. The tail-lights narrowed to two red points, then four, then none. The pine trees swallowed the road entirely.

Art stayed at the fence until the sound of the cylinders died away. His hands were numb from the iron bars. When he finally turned back toward the workshop, he saw Leo staring down at the tablet screen. The indicator was still solid green. The baseline had been restored. But the air on the street felt thin, cold, and entirely empty.

Systems Panoramic

The external security routine for Sub-District 4-A initialized its overnight infrared scan pattern across the southern approach zone. Registering no moving thermal signatures greater than fifteen kilograms within the forty-meter boundary, the primary processor reduced its power state by twelve percent. The system log recorded a status of absolute spatial isolation at twenty-one point zero zero hours.

PART IV:
THE BLACKOUT

Chapter 14:
The Brittleness Debt Comes Due

Systems Panoramic

Over eleven fiscal years, the sector removed all non-essential redundancy from its water storage, power routing, and medical supply architecture. Mean service efficiency increased across each reporting quarter. Reserve capacity fell to zero. For thirty-six months, the system registered improved output with no visible instability. At zero point twelve hours, an electrical discharge carrying thirty kiloamperes struck a high-voltage transmission tower half a mile outside the sector perimeter. The resulting surge entered a network with no alternate channel left available to absorb load. Failure propagated at full system speed.

Scene Core (Leo POV)

Leo woke to the smell of scorching fiberglass. It was a dry, chemical stench that hit the back of the throat like acid, layered over the familiar smell of warm dust and battery plastic that the garage usually carried after a long day of charging cycles. This was sharper. Hotter. Wrong.

The tablet on the nightstand was flashing a continuous crimson alert sequence:

BANK 1 THERMAL RUNAWAY.
OVERTEMPERATURE DETECTED.

Leo threw off the blanket and swung their legs to the floor. The loft boards were cold under bare feet, but the air below was hot enough to rise through the gaps in the planks. When they yanked open the loft door and tore down the stairs, a smear of gray smoke was already pushing along the ceiling joists of the main work area in layered bands.

The workbench lights were still on, but dimming in pulses. Behind the partition wall, the primary inverter stack was emitting a high-pitched whine that sounded like a circular saw hitting a knot of pine. The aluminum battery casing ticked and flexed from internal heat. A yellow wrench lying on the bench vibrated in place from the resonance.

"Leo!" Elena shouted, slamming the cellar door behind her. She had a wool blanket held over her nose and mouth. Her coat was half-zipped, one sleeve inside out where she had dragged it on too fast. "The master display on my porch just died. The electronic locks on the food storage bays are rattling."

Leo dropped into the chair at the auxiliary keyboard. The keys felt hot, slick with condensed humidity. "The surge crossed the communication line," they said, fingers moving across the manual override screen. "The lightning arrestor we couldn't replace in April leaked the charge straight into the charging bus. Bank One is venting at two hundred and eighty-four degrees Fahrenheit and climbing."

They hit the isolation sequence. The green status text broke into vertical bands of white static, then re-formed on a single frozen line:

Command Timeout. Relay Stalled in Closed State.

"The automated relay fused," Leo said, reaching for the dry chemical extinguisher with one hand while trying the override again with the other. "It won't open. The current is looping through the cells, and the cooling fans are dead because the auxiliary fuse blew during the first strike."

A dull, heavy pop echoed from the battery casing. The sheet metal buckled outward by two inches. A jet of white lithium smoke hissed through the rivet holes and curled toward the rafters with a sweet, poisonous smell like burned solvent.

Elena grabbed Leo by the shoulder and hauled them backward. "Out of the garage. Now. If those cells breach the outer casing, the vapor will take the rafters with it."

They stumbled into the driveway under a sky full of violent light. Rain hit so hard it seemed to come sideways, each drop cold enough to sting. Purple lightning sheeted over the neighborhood in bursts, turning the cul-de-sac into a series of hard black-and-white images, the fence, the barrels, the greenhouses, the open cellar doors, the wet backs of people already waking to crisis.

Art was already at the wellhead, but his heavy pipe wrench was sitting idle in the mud by his boots. He was staring down the dark length of Silverbrook Road, his hands buried deep in the pockets of his yellow slicker, his shoulders rounded against the freezing rain. For a moment he looked less like a mechanic than like a man listening for something he had already heard once before.

When Leo shouted his name, Art did not move for three seconds. Then his hands came out of his pockets and hovered over the iron handle of the manual backup lever, not quite touching it.

"The automated line is foaming, Art!" Leo yelled, wiping rain out of their eyes with the back of a bare wrist.

Art looked down at the mud, his jaw tightening until the old scar along his cheek turned white. He picked up the wrench, his grip slipping once on the wet iron before he could set the teeth against the casing. "We let the line go," he said. Then he drove the handle down hard against the wellhead assembly.

"The automated pump isn't cycling," Art shouted over the thunder. "The solenoid valve is stuck."

Leo looked down at the tablet in their hand. The screen was black now. The internal receiver had fried when the garage router melted. The digital dashboard was gone. The network map was gone. The clean lattice of indicators that had once made the street feel knowable had collapsed into dead glass.

"The turbidity sensor," Leo whispered. Rain ran down over their lips and into their mouth. "The sediment from the storm. The sensor didn't calibrate. It's blind."

"It isn't blind, boy. It's dead," Art said. He knelt in the mud and hammered the wrench against the seized assembly until the casing rang like struck pipe. "The fine clay slurry from the drawdown has been packing into the valve seat for weeks because your script skipped the manual flush. The surge locked the solenoid wide open while the well was pulling gray mud from the bottom invert."

Leo dropped to the sight-tube line and wiped the plastic with the heel of a wet palm. Through it, the fluid moving through the domestic pipe was no longer water in any ordinary sense. It was thick, opaque, and the color of wet cement, streaked with darker ribbons of iron bacteria and floating grit.

Their stomach tightened. Yesterday the dashboard had shown clear flow, stable pressure, nominal status. Yesterday every number had still been green.

"It's in the distribution lines," Leo said. "The software didn't close the gate valves before the power died. The mud is inside the storage tanks for every house on the street."

A scream rose from somewhere across the cul-de-sac, followed by the metallic chatter of a faucet spitting grit.

Porch lights that had been running on backup inverters winked out one by one. Doors opened. Flashlight beams began to slash across the muddy roadbed in frantic arcs. People stepped into the rain holding buckets, mugs, and stripped-down lanterns, not looking at dashboards anymore, not waiting for alerts, just listening to the sick noise their plumbing was making.

Across the lane, old habits were still firing a few seconds behind reality. Mrs. Albright stood on her porch stabbing at the blank face of her wall monitor as if one more touch might produce an alert telling her what to do. A man from House 3 kept lifting and lowering the dead smart-tank lid, waiting for the automatic purge cycle that would never come. Near the storage bay, one of the selected refugees from the convoy was already cranking the fused keypad housing with a screwdriver, not to fix it exactly but because his hands still believed every locked thing had a code path back to order. The infrastructure had failed at machine speed. The people inside it were failing more slowly, by reflex.

From the garage came another muffled pop. The smoke thickened at the roofline. Behind Leo, Elena was already shouting for blankets, for sand, for somebody to kill the breaker at the secondary panel even if the labels were wrong.

The neighborhood had spent months believing it was being monitored. In one storm, the instruments burned away and the real machinery lay exposed, raw and dirty, in their hands.

Systems Panoramic

The localized data network for Sub-District 4-A experienced a total architectural collapse at zero point thirty-two hours. The thirty-two residential monitoring nodes ceased all data transmission, leaving the central processor in a permanent loop state. The physical infrastructure, unmonitored, uncalibrated, and over-optimized, was left completely exposed to the raw hydrological force of the rising water table.

Chapter 15:
The Convergence Climax

Systems Panoramic

The volumetric capacity of the primary distribution reservoir dropped to twelve percent efficiency as four thousand liters of unfiltered sediment settled into the domestic lines. At the southern approach, a sustained infrared signature indicating fifty-two human bodies reassumed a stationary position sixty meters from the iron perimeter. The administrative sector network remained zero percent active.

Scene Core (Elena POV)

Elena kept her palm pressed against the cold iron of the gatehouse wall. Her left eye was swollen shut from an hour spent in the mud under House 3, trying to close an unlabeled copper bypass valve by headlamp. The skin across her knuckles was split where the wrench had slipped. Rainwater kept finding the cuts and making them sting fresh each time she tightened her grip. The air on the street tasted of sulfur, wet clay, and the bitter copper tang of water that had sat too long in rusted municipal iron.

Nothing in the cul-de-sac was where it belonged anymore. Buckets stood in the road catching brown runoff from burst gutter seams. The storage bay doors remained sealed, the fused strike plate still dead in its housing. Two children were wrapped in blankets on Elena's porch with enamel bowls beside them. At the far end of the lane, men were taking turns on the hand pump because the settlement tank could no longer be trusted to draw evenly on its own. Somewhere beyond the garages, Art and the others were still in the mud at the wellhead, shouting measurements over the rain and the racket of seized hardware.

"The Davis family has two kids purging on the kitchen floor," Sarah said. She stood in the downpour with her nurse's apron soaked through, her fingers twitching over the handle of an empty water canvas. Wet hair had come loose from its tie and stuck to her jaw. "The sediment got into their secondary storage tank before the manual isolation valve jammed. If we don't get clean water to flush their systems by noon, the dehydration will lock their kidneys. The youngest was already running ragged from the ear infection after we cut their medical access last week."

Elena looked past Sarah to her own porch. One of the bowls tipped, rolled, and rang once against the step before settling upside down in the water. "The storage bay doors are sealed," she said, her voice dropping into the low, flat register she had used on ER floors when mass casualty triage was already overtaking staffing. "The electronic strike plate fused in the surge. We can't get to the grain sacks or the rehydration salts without an iron sledge, and Henderson has half the council at the well telling people I knew the sensors were drifting."

As if on cue, Miller came running down the middle of the muddy cul-de-sac from the northern fence, carrying a rusted crowbar. Soot streaked one cheek from the garage fire. He was breathing through his mouth, too fast to speak cleanly at first, and his boots threw fan-shaped spray with every step.

"The council is meeting by the wellhead," he said when he got close enough to stop. "Henderson is telling everyone your family should lose the keys and the storage rights. He says if we wait another hour, we'll have a riot on the street."

"Let them vote," Elena said. She did not turn toward the well. She was looking through the iron bars of the southern gate, where the headlights of two delivery vans had just flickered back to life through the rain.

The convoy had returned.

The vehicles did not stop sixty meters back this time. They rolled forward until the front bumper of Marcus's lead van was six inches from the iron chain. Mud sucked at the tires. The doors opened almost in sequence. Thirty people climbed out into the rain, not an abstract convoy of nodes but a line of hollow-cheeked neighbors from the next district, wrapped in wet blankets, carrying fuel cans, tool bags, dented cook pots, and children too tired to cry. One man limped with a door hinge slung over his shoulder. A woman got out with both hands around a sealed plastic drum as if she had been carrying it for days without setting it down.

Marcus Calder walked to the center of the line. He didn't have his clipboard now. He had a five-gallon iron fuel can in his right hand and a length of threaded black pipe in his left. His reflective vest hung open, dark with rain, and his swollen bad leg dragged hard enough through the gravel to leave a shallow groove. He looked less like an administrator than like a man who had stripped a dead plant for whatever practical pieces were left.

"The high school camp was empty, Elena," Marcus said through the mesh. Rain ran through his gray stubble and dripped off his chin onto the collar of the vest. "The federal trucks never came. We sat forty-eight hours in an unheated gymnasium with no water while the children got worse. We are coming inside the perimeter now."

Elena stepped straight up to the line until her face was inches from his. "We have no clean water, Marcus. The well is contaminated with gray silt. The automated filters are fried, and our own people are starting to purge on the floor. If I open this gate without terms, I am not saving anyone. I am widening the failure."

For a second Marcus said nothing. Behind him, one of the former plant operators knelt and unrolled a canvas kit on the hood of the van to keep it out of the mud. Even in the rain, Elena could make out the shapes inside: valve picks, packing hooks, sealant, brass brushes, wrapped copper mesh, hand files. They had not come as petitioners only. They had come with labor and parts.

Henderson came down the lane with four neighbors carrying timber balks on their shoulders. His face was white with anger and lack of sleep. The men behind him spread slightly as they approached, not quite a formation but close enough to register as one.

"We aren't letting the people who want to steal what's left of our dry food inside this line, Elena," Henderson said. "You're the one who signed the triage order two nights ago."

She turned just far enough to answer him. "I signed an algorithm, Henderson. I let a screen do the choosing. That was mine. I am opening this gate, and if the grain drops, it drops from my hand, not the machine's."

The words landed in the rain and stayed there. Miller looked from her to the convoy and back again. Sarah lowered the empty canvas bag.

Elena turned back to Marcus and began counting on her fingers, not because she needed help remembering, but because the terms had to exist in air before they could exist in any ledger. "If I open this lock, your operators go straight into the mud with Art. No allocations. No special rations for your families. Your people carry wood, clear sand beds, strip the fouled lines, and pull night watch on the boiling stations. We split grain by mouths, not hours, and we run all of it by the ledger on the bench. If anyone touches the storage cage without the porch count, the gate closes again. If anybody lies about tools, water, or fuel, the work detail loses draw priority at evening ration."

Marcus listened without interrupting. Rain ran off the pipe in his hand and drummed on the gravel. "We brought four rolls of copper mesh and two cases of mechanical gaskets from the plant maintenance shed," he said. "One of my operators can rebuild the secondary check seat if Art still has a lathe. Another can hand-clear the fouled flush line if you have chain and a pull handle. We also brought two drums of diesel cut with kerosene. Not clean, but it will burn."

He set the iron can down first, then lowered the pipe to the gravel. "Open the chain."

No one moved. Rain hammered the sheet metal roofs. Somewhere behind Elena, a child retched into a basin on her porch. At the wellhead, somebody shouted for another wrench. The whole cul-de-sac was trying not to come apart faster than the people inside it could think.

For a moment it seemed the whole street might choose the worst available answer all at once. One of Henderson's men shifted the timber balk off his shoulder and took two steps toward the storage bay as if securing grain mattered more than water now. Miller tightened both hands on the crowbar and looked not at Marcus but at the sealed doors behind Elena's porch. Sarah moved instinctively toward the

Davis house, then stopped midway, caught between the children on the kitchen floor and the argument at the gate. Even the admitted four from the earlier selection had come up from the work sheds and were standing off to one side, watching with the strained stillness of people who knew they could become targets from either direction. The cul-de-sac had narrowed to a final minute before inward collapse.

Elena reached into her pocket, pulled out the iron key to the master padlock, and dropped it into Henderson's palm. The metal hit his skin with a small, unmistakable click.

"Unlock it," she said. "Then go to my house and tell your wife to get the copper pots ready. From this hour on, we boil everything that comes out of the ground."

Systems Panoramic

The mechanical latch on the southern gate dropped into its open position at eleven point forty-five hours as forty pounds of human force threw the iron frame back against the gravel. The spatial isolation status for Sub-District 4-A terminated. The local ecosystem shifted from a closed technical loop to an open human order, registering an immediate consumption spike of three hundred percent against zero working data streams.

Chapter 16:
The Hierarchy Inverted

Systems Panoramic

The local mesh network registered twenty-four operational data nodes across the expanded sector perimeter. The central processor converted repaired solar-panel current into standard digital logs. The optimization modules remained deactivated, their code strings archived in a read-only subdirectory. The system functioned as a monitoring array only, recording structural metrics without administrative intervention.

Scene Core (Leo POV)

Leo used a piece of fine sandpaper to clean the ash deposits from the copper terminal block of the master inverter. The garage smelled of scorched plastic, damp lime from the floorboards, and the boiled starch scent of potato water cooling in large zinc tubs by the door. Every few strokes, the abrasive paper gave off a dry metallic whisper, and a faint crescent of black residue gathered on Leo's thumb.

The workbench had changed shape over the past month without anyone formally deciding it would. The old battery diagnostics sheets were gone. In their place sat a stack of hand-ruled census ledgers weighted with a brass valve body, a chipped enamel mug full of sharpened carpentry pencils, and two cloth sacks of cleaned washers sorted by diameter. Someone had driven three small finishing nails into the wall above the monitor to hang the current week's handwritten water totals. The room looked less like a control station now and more like a shop that happened to contain a screen.

The monitor was alive again, but the screen layout was unrecognizable. The gold banners, predictive scatter plots, and automated allocation alerts were gone. In their place sat a single, flat terminal window displaying three lines of raw text:

Well Intake: 14 Liters/Min.
Turbidity: 1.1 NTU.
Battery State: 42% (Manual Charge Control).

The machine had been reduced to something honest.

Leo checked the inverter screws one by one with a stubby insulated driver, not because the system had flagged a fault, but because Art had said the rebuilt terminal would loosen if the garage warmed too fast after rain. The screws held. Leo wiped the fine copper dust off the bench with the edge of their sleeve and listened to the room. Somewhere outside, a hand pump squealed twice. From Elena's porch came the low, overlapping murmur of people negotiating evening water shares. A baby cried once, then stopped. Someone laughed without finding anything funny in it.

"The software update is stable," Leo said, not looking up as the cellar door creaked.

Eli Davis, Toby's older brother from House 7, whose family had been penalized by the old audit code, walked into the garage. He wasn't carrying a tablet. He had a heavy leather-bound accounting ledger tucked under his arm and a stub of carpentry pencil behind his ear. There was mud dried to the cuff of one pant leg and a pale line on his forearm where the morning bucket handle had pressed into the skin. He sat down on an overturned crate next to Leo, opening the book across his knees with the careful, flat-palmed touch people used around things that mattered now.

"The morning water census from the northern sector is complete," Eli Davis said, his finger tracking a row of hand-written ink numbers on the paper page. "The three houses on the ridge used forty-two gallons total for the garden flush. Write that down into the log."

Leo typed the numbers into the terminal window, the keys clicking softly in the quiet room. The entry form was blunt by design: time, source, quantity, remarks. No projections. No recommendations. No hidden adjustments waiting behind a confirm button. "The database has it," Leo said. "The storage tank should hit full capacity by sixteen hundred if the solar pumps keep their current velocity."

Eli looked at the corner of the screen where the old allocation prompts used to appear. Nothing flashed. No color warning climbed the margin. "The code doesn't write the ticket, right?" he asked.

Leo kept their voice even. "The code only counts the gallons now. The allocation is written in your book. If the Davis house needs an extra two gallons for the pediatric rinse tonight, the script won't drop your family's flour ration tomorrow morning to balance the curve. Elena handles the variance on the porch."

Eli nodded once, but his mouth tightened before he looked back to the ledger. "My mother still won't come up your porch steps unless Sarah is already there," he said, not accusingly, just as a fact that had learned how to live in the house. "She says the boards remember the day Toby came back with the empty bucket."

Through the cracked side window came Elena's voice, flatter now from overuse, reading off the evening draw to three households clustered under her porch awning. A man objected to the bucket count from the ridge houses. Elena asked who had carried the extra water up the slope. Someone answered. Someone else corrected the answer. Paper shifted. Pencil scratched. The disagreement did not disappear. It got measured, spoken, and assigned.

Leo looked down at their own hands, where the skin around the knuckles was still raw and faintly yellowed from the battery acid cleanup. A burn mark ran along the side of the right wrist where the fused relay housing had brushed them during the storm. They remembered the pristine clarity of the old optimization matrix, the sense of safety that had come from watching the green line graph project ninety days of absolute security. It had been a beautiful illusion. The code had balanced perfectly because it had treated human survival as a mathematical certainty, ignoring the friction of clay in the well, the real sickness in the houses, and the fact that people did not stay inside their assigned columns.

The cellar door opened again, and Art walked in carrying a brass packing gland he had spent the morning machining on the manual lathe in his cellar. His overalls were black with grease, the knees dark with dried mud, and the cuff of one sleeve was stiff where old sealant had cured into the fabric. He set the part on the bench with the care of a man putting down something that had taken time to get right.

"The secondary filter bed has twelve inches of clean sand in it," Art said. "Marcus and his boys finished the manual back-flush on the main line. The water coming through the sight-glass is clear enough to read a newspaper through."

Leo pulled a narrow strip of paper from the small printer on the shelf. It wasn't an allocation slip, just a raw data sheet showing the optical clarity measurements from the wellhead sensor over the past six hours. The sensor had survived, but only as an instrument, no longer as judge. "The sensor matches your manual check," Leo said, handing him the printout. "The turbidity curve flattened at one point one. The optical lens is clean."

Art didn't look at the paper. He took the pencil from behind Eli's ear, reached over the workbench, and wrote a single line directly onto the wooden surface beneath the monitor:

Filter 2: Re-sanded May 21. Max flow 15 GPM. Check the manual seals every Tuesday.

The graphite bit into the grain and held there. Leo watched the letters darken the wood. The terminal beside them continued to display its neat digital readings, but the actual instruction, the one that would keep the line working when the power failed again, was now sitting in plain sight where no surge could erase it.

"The screen will go dark again the next time a lightning tower takes a hit," Art said, his voice dropping into that low craftsman register that left no room for debate. "But the wood doesn't blink. Keep your data on the paper and your hands on the valves. The machine is a good tool for telling you how fast the water is moving, but it's a rotten master for telling you who gets to drink it."

From the porch came Elena's voice again, this time more tired than sharp. A bucket was reassigned. Someone accepted less than they had asked for. Someone else objected to getting more because it would look like favoritism tomorrow. No speaker settled the matter cleanly. The settlement happened in the back-and-forth itself. The work of fairness had slowed down enough to become visible again.

Leo rested their fingers on the plastic frame of the monitor. They had spent months trying to code human bias out of the cul-de-sac, only to watch the tool they built turn hard under scarcity. The new arrangement was slower, messier, and impossible to automate cleanly. It required arguments on porches, revisions in ledgers, and adults willing to say aloud which burden they were choosing to carry. But it was anchored in the earth. The code was no longer the authority. It was one instrument on a bench full of tools that could fail.

Systems Panoramic

The distribution valves along the primary residential line adjusted their positions via manual lever adjustments carried out by forty-two individual citizens during the afternoon census. The centralized server recorded the flow rates as static inputs, updating the local storage metrics without generating a single system correction command. The community log file remained one hundred percent active, tracking the physical stability of the parallel loop through the medium of human labor.

Chapter 17:
Passing the Codex

Systems Panoramic

The solar elevation over Sub-District 4-A reached zero degrees at nineteen point thirty hours, terminating the direct current generation from the roof arrays. The local mesh transmitter decreased its signal frequency to three point five megahertz, adjusting its transmission pattern to utilize the atmospheric ionization layer over the Atlantic coast line. The regional grid remained dark across nine hundred square kilometers.

Scene Core (Art POV)

Art sat on the high three-legged stool by his cedar workbench, watching the oil lamp flame flicker behind its glass chimney. The room was cold, but the air was still, smelling of linseed oil, graphite, and the sharp tallow scent of the lamp wick.

Open on the grease-stained wood before him was the leather-bound ledger. The pages were stiff, rippled into thick waves from the floodwater that had soaked them during the blackout, the margins dense with forty years of ink calculations, hydraulic formulas, and hand-drawn cross-sections of subterranean valves.

Leo sat on the low packing crate beside the bench, a fresh notebook open across their knees. Leo's fingers were dark with graphite dust, their thumb stained with the blue ink of a manual fountain pen. They were physically copying Art's 1998 schematic for a double-check backflow preventer, drawing the lines millimeter by millimeter with an old celluloid ruler.

The wood didn't blink. The paper didn't lose its cache when the voltage dropped.

"Keep the radius on the casing seat tight, Leo," Art said, pointing the blunt end of his wire brush at the pencil line on Leo's page. "If you leave more than a sixty-fourth of an inch of play in that housing, the grit will wedge behind the flap the first time the well pump draws vacuum. The diagram shows the clearance under load. Don't smooth it out to make the drawing look pretty."

Leo didn't look up from the page. They drew a small, dark crescent curve where the rubber gasket met the brass seat, their pen scratching softly against the coarse grain of the paper. "The digital translation is ready for the packet loop. I have the filtration dimensions coded into three hundred bytes of raw text."

"The text doesn't matter if they don't have the leather to cut the washers, boy," Art said. He reached over, picked up the old ledger, and closed the cover with a heavy, deliberate thud that sent a small puff of cedar dust into the light of the lamp. He slid the book across the oil-stained wood until it rested against Leo's forearm. "Take it. The ink won't smear if you keep the grease off the bindings. It belongs in the garage now."

Leo touched the worn hide of the cover, their thumb tracing the deep scar where a pipe wrench had gouged the leather twenty years ago. They did not say thank you. They simply took the book, holding it against their ribs like a piece of salvaged hardware.

The door to the yard opened, and Elena walked into the workshop. She carried a cold, unlit hand-cranked lantern in her left hand, her winter coat zipped to her jaw against the evening chill. She walked to the window, looking out toward the ridge line where Leo's directional copper antenna was pointed through the pine branches.

"The battery storage in the garage is sitting at thirty-eight percent," Elena said. Her voice had none of the flat, spreadsheet certainty of the winter months; it was quiet, rough from a day spent negotiating grain distributions with the Davis family on her porch. "If we throw the switch on the transmitter, we drop our domestic lighting reserve by two hours. We won't have enough power to run the clinic monitors tomorrow morning if the sun doesn't clear the mist by eight."

Leo looked up from the bench, their hand still resting on Art's ledger. "The transmission code is short, Elena. It takes ninety seconds to push the water schematics across the high-frequency band. If we don't send it tonight, the cold front tomorrow will drop the ionosphere before our next window."

Elena looked from Leo's face to the dark silhouette of the transmitter housing on the shelf. She knew the arithmetic of the choice. Sending the signal meant exposing their location to anyone still scanning the bands between here and Richmond. It meant broadcasting knowledge into a world that had already shown how desperate it could be. It was risk without clean return.

"Turn the dial," Elena said. She set the hand-cranked lantern on the desk and reached out to hold the window frame as the wind rattled the glass. "Send the line."

Leo stood up, stepped to the shelf, and threw the heavy knife-switch.

The green LED on the transmitter face didn't glow with the bright, stable light of the old dashboard system; it flickered rapidly, a low-voltage, unstable pulse that hummed in the quiet of the shop. The speaker emitted a dry, continuous rush of static that sounded like dry leaves scraping across concrete.

Leo pressed the brass key, their fingers sending the packet in a brief, rhythmic sequence of clicks:

Lorton 4-A. Sand filter schematic available. Aqua baseline stable. Frequency 3.5.

The signal went out into the dark—a fragile, low-power burst of digital text riding on an analog wave, scratching against the immense silence of the continent.

The screen on Leo's terminal remained blank. The static hissed through the speaker, unyielding and cold. For two minutes, the three of them stood in the yellow light of the oil lamp, listening to the dead air of a collapsed infrastructure.

Then, the speaker didn't chime. The software didn't register a handshake.

But on the bottom line of the terminal window, a single row of distorted gray pixels crawled across the screen. The text was garbled, broken by the atmospheric discharge of the storm over the mountains, dropping characters like debris in a current.

...R_C_V... S_T_A_B_L... N_O_D_E_7...

The characters froze, stayed live on the glass for four seconds, and then drowned in a fresh wave of white noise as the transmission line dropped out.

Leo stared at the broken letters. It wasn't an alliance. It wasn't aid. It was proof: somewhere beyond the black ridge and the dead cities, someone else was still awake, still trying to keep water moving clean through a damaged line.

Art walked back to the stove, took the iron poker, and adjusted the log until the wood caught, throwing a fresh circle of amber light across the floorboards. He did not celebrate. He looked at Leo, then at Elena, his face settled into the quiet, permanent lines of a man who had finally stopped running from his choices.

"Get your pencil back out, Leo," Art said, his voice level in the shadows. "The valve on the secondary settlement tank is going to need a new washer by Tuesday morning. Write down the dimensions before the lamp goes out."

Systems Panoramic

The external security routine for Sub-District 4-A shifted to its low-frequency cycle as solar radiation dropped to zero. Registering no electronic updates or administrative check-ins from the regional core, the sector logs remained frozen at twenty-three point fifty-nine hours. The local loop functioned as an unmapped independent cell, balancing survival through the unrecorded physical needs of thirty-four distinct human bodies.

www.ingramcontent.com/pod-product-compliance
Lightning Source LLC
LaVergne TN
LVHW010840120826
845149LV00017B/3319

* 9 7 9 8 9 9 6 2 1 8 7 1 4 *

FAILURE
IS NOT AN OPTION

A BLUEPRINT FOR AN UNBREAKABLE MENTALITY

COREY A. COWART JR.

Build A Brother
PUBLISHING